"Sit down!" His quiet words were a command

Something in his ruggedly handsome features warned Sherry not to disobey.

"Tell me about David," Rollo said in that frighteningly quiet voice. "Tell me about my son, Sherry . . . and don't insult me by telling me he's not my son," he added harshly. "My God, why didn't you tell me you were pregnant?"

"You said no commitments. Remember?" she said. "Would you have married me just to make an honest woman of me? No, thank you!"

"My child's entitled to my name, and I'll make sure he gets it."

Fear placed its icy hand over her heart. "What are you talking about?"

"I took your virginity, and in the process helped to make him." He bit out the words. "We're going to be married, whether you like it or not. Do I make myself clear?"

Yvonne Whittal, a born dreamer, started scribbling stories at an early age but admits she's glad she didn't have to make her living by writing then. "Otherwise," she says, "I would surely have starved!" After her marriage and the birth of three daughters, she began submitting short stories to publishers. Now she derives great satisfaction from writing full-length books. The characters become part of Yvonne's life in the process, so much so that she almost hates coming to the end of each manuscript and having to say farewell to dear and trusted friends.

Books by Yvonne Whittal

HARLEQUIN ROMANCE

HARLEQUIN PRESENTS

This One
Night
Yvonne Whittal

Harlequin Books

TORONTO • NEW YORK • LONDON
AMSTERDAM • PARIS • SYDNEY • HAMBURG
STOCKHOLM • ATHENS • TOKYO • MILAN

Original hardcover edition published in 1986
by Mills & Boon Limited

ISBN 0-373-17010-6

Harlequin Romance first edition March 1987

CHAPTER ONE

'WHAT do you mean you're not coming? You've just got to come, Sherry!' Brenda Lewis wailed over the telephone. 'It's my twenty-first birthday, and it's going to be a swinging party.'

Sherry Jaeger sighed tiredly and she could not control the tremor in her hands when she unnecessarily straightened the skirt of her nursing uniform. She was well acquainted with Brenda's swinging parties, and she detested them. The mere thought of having to be a part of all that rowdy hilarity made her cringe inwardly. A patient in her ward had died that morning; it was someone she had been extremely fond of, and she would have preferred to spend the evening alone at home to weep the tears she had had to control all day, but she also could not ignore the fact that it was Brenda's twenty-first birthday.

'I'll come,' Sherry agreed reluctantly, and she hastily ended the conversation when she looked up to see the matron entering the duty-room.

'Mr Peterson's family is at the reception office. They've come to collect his personal things,' Matron Naudé announced. 'Will you see to it, Sister Jaeger?'

Sherry nodded, her face rigid with the effort to hide her unhappiness at the task she had to perform, and her pace was brisk when she walked out of the duty-room. A man had died, she thought with a measure of disgust as she walked away, but everything simply continued as if nothing had happened. His family might pause to mourn his passing, but the organised, highly efficient routine in Cape Town's general hospital never faltered for a second. After five years of nursing she still found herself wondering at a time like this whether she had chosen the right profession.

Sherry deliberately arrived a half-hour late at Brenda's flat that evening to avoid the initial crush. The din emerging from behind the closed door was enough to make her want to turn on her heel and run. Amazed that the neighbours never complained, she squared her shoulders instead, and went inside. Her ears were subjected to instant torture. The recorded music was loud, the volume of the base had been turned up until the floor seemed to vibrate beneath Sherry's feet, and thirty or more voices seemed to be vying against the twanging of electric guitars.

The noise was jarring, and she glanced about her nervously, her grey glance scanning the sea of familiar faces, but in this rowdy environment she could do no more than raise her hand in a casual greeting, and she was extraordinarily relieved when Brenda appeared beside her in a full-length emerald green evening-gown which accentuated the alabaster smoothness of her skin and the paleness of her long silky hair.

'I was beginning to think you'd let me down!' Brenda shouted to make herself heard above the music when Sherry had handed her a gift and had wished her a happy birthday. 'I have something to tell you.' She literally dragged Sherry into the nearest bedroom and closed the door to obliterate some of the noise. Excitement sparkled in her hazel eyes and made her lovely features glow as if a light had been lit inside her.

Sherry stared at her friend, and a dreadful suspicion suddenly spiralled through her. 'Don't tell me you're pregnant.'

'I am!' Brenda laughed into Sherry's shocked face. 'But there's more to tell you. Jonathan and I were married this morning, so this is actually a triple celebration.'

Relief washed over Sherry and her tense body relaxed a fraction. 'I'm so glad.'

'I knew you would be,' Brenda laughed again, her

small teeth flashing white against her crimson lips. 'You never did like the idea of Jonathan and me simply living together.'

'I know you think I'm a prude.'

'But you're a nice prude,' Brenda corrected soberly, her glance taking in Sherry's perfectly oval face with the small straight nose, and the full, sensitive mouth. 'That's why you're the first to hear our wonderful news.'

Sherry felt strangely honoured, and tears stung her eyelids when she embraced Brenda. 'I'm so happy for both you and Jonathan.'

'Let's go out there and enjoy ourselves,' Brenda laughed away her own tears, and Sherry was once again plunged into the midst of the rowdy party. 'The eats and drinks are on the tables against the opposite wall,' Brenda enlightened her. 'Help yourself whenever you feel like it.'

Sherry elbowed her way across the room, but Jonathan Hunt, tall and lean with laughing brown eyes, caught her arm and swung her into the disco beat before she could protest. She was not in the mood for this wild dancing, but courtesy made her sway somewhat reluctantly in a milder version of the cavorting dance.

Jonathan pulled her closer unexpectedly and put his mouth close to her ear to make himself heard. 'Has Brenda given you the good news?'

'Yes,' she answered stiffly. 'Congratulations.'

'Does it make you like me a little better?'

'I've never disliked you, Jonathan,' Sherry protested with inherent honesty. 'I simply never liked what you and Brenda were doing with your lives.'

His hands released her, and she almost shouted with relief when the music came to a crashing halt. She excused herself hastily, but she had barely reached the other side of the room when the twanging of guitars reverberated through the room once again. She helped herself to a glass of wine and shrank into the furthest corner of the lounge, close to the balcony. There was no escape from the noise, but the balcony doors stood open, and she did at least have the pleasure of the occasional breath of fresh air as it wafted into the smoke-filled room.

The evening stretched ahead of Sherry like an endless torment. She sipped her wine and leaned against the cool wall, but her slender body would not relax. Too much had happened that day, and her heart and her mind rejected this gaiety. It was a hot January night, and Sherry raised a hand to brush a heavy strand of golden-brown hair away from her damp forehead. Her grey glance shifted aimlessly across the crowded room, then bounced back swiftly to the man leaning nonchalantly against the opposite wall beside Jonathan's metre-high statue of Venus. He had not been there a moment before, she could almost swear to that, but he was there *now*, and for some inexplicable reason she could not look away again.

His hair was dark, darker than her own, and he wore it cropped close to his nicely shaped head. His forehead was broad and intelligent above straight dark brows, and there was a hint of laziness in the heavy-lidded eyes. The nose was high-bridged and straight above the strongly chiselled mouth, and there was a suggestion of a dent in the square, resolute jaw. It was a strong face with plenty of character woven into its ruggedness and, when her glance slid from his wide shoulders down the long length of him to his polished shoes, she felt an odd tightness at the pit of her stomach. He turned his head as if he had sensed that he was being observed, and Sherry felt a wave of heat surging into her cheeks. Her embarrassment was obvious to him, she could see it in the way the corners of his mouth lifted in amusement, and she hastily lowered her dark lashes to hide the confusion which was pulsating through her when he raised his glass in a mocking salute.

He made no attempt to approach her as the evening wore on, but she became increasingly aware of the fact that *he* was now observing *her* intently, and her glance collided several times with that of the man with the rugged but striking good looks. She was helping herself to a second glass of wine and a snack when Brenda joined her, and Sherry took this opportunity to question her friend.

'Who's the man in the blue blazer and grey slacks?' she asked with careful casualness.

'Do you mean the one who's been propping up the wall next to Jonathan's statue of the goddess of love?'

'Yes, that's him,' Sherry confirmed.

'His name is Rollo something-or-other. He's an old acquaintance of Jonathan's, and Jonathan invited him along to the party.' Brenda eyed Sherry speculatively. 'Do you want an introduction?'

Sherry shook her head hastily. 'I was asking out of curiosity, not because I was angling for an introduction.'

'Well, it looks as if he's decided to come over and introduce himself,' Brenda remarked drily, casting a swift glance across the room before she faded away and left Sherry standing there with a pounding heart and legs that felt as if they were ready to cave in beneath her.

'It's quite a party,' a deep, well-modulated voice drawled behind her; taking a steadying breath, she turned slowly to face him.

'Yes, it is,' she acknowledged his statement, raising her glance no higher than the tanned column of his strong throat where his white shirt had been left unbuttoned.

The music went wild, and so did the writhing, bouncing bodies on the floor. Someone backed sharply into the man standing a pace away from Sherry, and the only thing which prevented him from cannoning into her was the swiftness with which he reached out to steady himself against the table. His action had, however, brought them closer together, and she raised her startled glance to find herself looking a long way up into two incredibly blue eyes. A tremor of shock raced through her, and it was followed swiftly by a stab of recognition. Recognition of what? she wondered frantically. She had

never seen this man before in her life, and yet she had the
oddest feeling that she knew him. His eyes, like two
bright hypnotic jewels, held hers captive, and everything
else around her seemed to fade into a mist of oblivion.
Seconds—or was it hours?—later, she succeeded in
tearing her glance from his, but her heart was beating
against her breastbone as if she had indulged in an
unaccustomed exertion.

The glass of wine was removed from her trembling
fingers, and the touch of his hand beneath her elbow sent
little darts of electricity shooting down into her fingers
and up into her shoulder. She was surprised when she
found herself standing out on the balcony overlooking
the moonlit sea, and she was not exactly sure how she had
got there.

There was nothing lazy now about his heavy-lidded
eyes while he studied her intently in the semi-darkness.
'Are you feeling better?' he asked.

She had no idea that she had been feeling ill, but being
out in the cool fresh air certainly made her feel a great
deal calmer.

'Did it appear to you as if I was going to faint, or
something equally drastic?' she counter-questioned
mockingly, leaning a little weakly against the glass door
while she tried desperately to regain her composure.

'You certainly went incredibly pale.' His heavy eyelids
were lowered to shade the expression in his eyes. 'Did
you see a ghost, or did I do something to frighten you?'

'Yes—no—I don't know.' She was stammering foolishly, and she groaned inwardly with embarrassment as
she turned away from him. 'I think I should go home.'

A blue-clad arm barred her way. 'My name is Rollo
van Cleef and, if it's any recommendation, Jonathan
Hunt and I have known each other since our university
days. A rowdy party isn't quite my idea of fun, but I
couldn't be impolite and turn down his invitation to this
particular celebration.' His arm dropped to his side,
giving her more room to breathe freely. 'I couldn't help

noticing that you haven't enjoyed this party either.'

'No, I haven't,' she confessed in a faintly breathless voice, and she wished fervently that he would not stand so close to her. She felt threatened by his tallness and the incredible width of his shoulders, and the woody scent of his masculine cologne stirred her senses until she felt incapable of thinking clearly.

'What's your name?' his deep voice questioned her above the noise coming from the lounge of Brenda's and Jonathan's flat.

'Sherry Jaeger.'

'Sherry.' He repeated her name slowly as if he was savouring it, and on his lips her name sounded like a caress. 'I like it. It's warm, subtle, and intoxicating, and I'm convinced that the silkiness of it matches the texture of your skin.'

There was a dangerous undercurrent of intimacy in that remark, and her fingers fluttered nervously against the flared skirt of her blue silk dress.

'I really must go, Mr van——'

'Rollo,' he corrected hastily, that blue-clad arm barring her way once again when she turned from him. 'We've only this minute introduced ourselves, and I'm afraid I can't let you go just yet.'

'But I must!' she protested frantically. 'It's almost midnight.'

His mouth twitched, and his brilliant blue eyes glittered with mockery. 'Tell me, Cinderella, will your coach turn into a pumpkin if you don't leave the party before the stroke of midnight?'

'Don't be silly!'

'Sherry . . .' His hand slid from the door to rest on her shoulder, and it felt as if every nerve in her body had suddenly become centred on that spot where his warm fingers touched her bare skin. 'I know a quiet little coffee bar about a block away from here.'

Sherry was momentarily speechless and also panicky. Something warned her that she had to stay away from this man who was having such an incredibly disturbing effect on her. 'Please, I must go home, and I——'

'They make excellent coffee, and they're open all night.' His fingers moved in a deliberate, persuasive caress against the silky smoothness of her shoulder, and a trembling weakness invaded her limbs. 'Are you tempted to join me there for a cup of coffee before I take you home?'

She was *tempted* to refuse, but the cacophony of sound that emerged from the flat was suddenly more than her tortured ears would continue to tolerate and, out of sheer desperation to escape the noise, she heard herself saying, 'I'll come with you.'

His hand fell away from her shoulder and a faintly triumphant smile curved his sensuous mouth. 'Say your farewells and I'll meet you at the door.'

Sherry turned from him on shaky legs and ploughed her way through the crowd to collect her wrap and evening bag. When she finally managed to find Brenda she saw a flicker of disappointment flash across her friend's face.

'Don't tell me you're going already?' she demanded.

'It's late and I've had a trying day,' Sherry defended herself, and she was relieved when Brenda accepted her explanation.

'I'll get Jonathan to run you home.'

'That won't be necessary,' Sherry assured her nervously. 'I'm leaving with Rollo van Cleef.'

'Oh!' Hazel eyes widened with curiosity, but Sherry said a hasty good night before Brenda could bombard her with questions.

Rollo van Cleef was waiting at the door as he had promised. His tall, muscular frame stepped towards her to take her arm, and suddenly she had grave doubts about her decision to accompany him to the coffee bar he had mentioned. His touch was awakening feelings she had not known that she possessed, and every time she looked into his eyes she had that disturbing sense of recognition.

He was a stranger to her. She had to continue telling herself that, but she could not rid herself entirely of the feeling that she knew him. Was this perhaps the crazy aftermath of an exhausting day at the hospital?

Sherry welcomed the cool sea breeze that blew up against her when they stepped out of the building, and the silence on the Clifton beach front was almost eerie after the noise in Brenda's flat.

'If you're having doubts about your decision to have coffee with me, then don't.' Rollo displayed an uncanny knack of gauging her thoughts. 'Molesting women is not one of my vices.'

Sherry glanced up at him quickly, and her cheeks felt warm when she looked away again. 'I didn't think you were the type to molest a woman, but a girl can't be too careful these days.'

'I'll grant you that,' he laughed shortly, then he changed the subject as they walked along the quiet, almost deserted street. 'Are you also in the nursing profession?'

'Yes, I am,' she confessed. 'Brenda and I studied together, although she came a little after me, and we shared a flat for a time until we decided to each get a place of our own.'

'Did sharing a flat put a strain on your friendship?'

'Not at first.' She had never before discussed her reasons for choosing not to share a flat with Brenda, but with Rollo van Cleef the truth simply spilled from her lips as if she did not have the power to prevent it. 'It was only when Brenda wanted to have Jonathan living in with us that the trouble started. I wouldn't agree to it, and we decided it would be best if we each found our own accommodation.'

Her explanation met with silence. Their shadows lengthened, shortened, and lengthened again each time they passed a street light. Had she perhaps said something wrong? Something to offend him?

'Do you object to a man and a woman living together

without being married?' Rollo questioned her at length,
and she glanced up at him quickly to see an amused smile
curving his mouth.

'I don't object to others doing so, if that's what they
want, but I don't want to be a part of it, and I don't
envisage that kind of life for myself.'

Oh, lord! She supposed she sounded so disgustingly
prim and proper that he must find it sickening, but for
some obscure reason she had to be honest with him.

'It's old-fashioned to believe that sex comes only after
marriage.'

'I know.' This was the second time within a space of
hours that she had stood accused of being old-fashioned.
'Brenda has called me a prude often enough, but I can't
help the way I feel about things, and I have no intention
of discarding my principles merely to please everyone
else.'

The fingers beneath her elbow tightened when they
reached the entrance to the coffee bar. She raised her
curious glance and was somewhat surprised to find that
Rollo van Cleef's expression was grave rather than
mocking.

'Stick to your principles, Sherry,' he said, his eyes
holding hers captive while the knuckles of his free hand
brushed like fire against her cool cheek. 'One day some
lucky man is going to love you all the more for it.'

His words triggered off an inexplicable sadness inside
her, and for one horrible moment she had the strangest
desire to burst into tears. She swallowed down the lump
in her throat, and he pushed open the door to usher her
into the coffee bar with its panelled walls and faintly
continental atmosphere.

It was after midnight, but a dozen or more people sat
hunched over a cup of steaming coffee while they
conversed quietly with their companions. The lighting
was soft, and the recorded music relayed through the
coffee bar was soothing after the ear-bashing Sherry had
received at Brenda's flat. Rollo chose a corner table and

ordered coffee.

'Tell me about yourself,' he prompted while they waited, and somehow Sherry found herself obeying him. Her father had died when she was eight years old, her mother had married again three years ago and had moved to Canada with her new husband, and she ended with the information that her brother was a doctor in Australia. It was perhaps a little crazy, but once she had started talking she could not stop, and she told him much more than she was sure he had wanted to know.

'I don't really know why I've been talking so much about myself to someone I've only just met,' she laughed self-consciously when their coffee arrived.

'It's often easier talking to a stranger about unimportant things while the true reason for our distress remains unspoken.'

His words struck a chord inside Sherry that filled her with pain and misery. It had been a long day; a day which had begun with the death of a friend and duties which had had to be performed despite her grief. She had wept all day behind the fixed smile she had presented to the other patients, and Brenda's riotous party had numbed her feelings temporarily, but Rollo van Cleef had intuitively placed a gentle finger on the raw wound.

Sherry blinked back the rush of tears and tried to laugh. 'Don't tell me you have psychic powers!'

'I spent a long time watching you this evening, and I knew it wasn't simply the rowdy party which was making you look so unhappy.' His hand covered hers on the checkered tablecloth and a comforting warmth flowed through her. 'Would you like to tell me about it?' his deep voice prompted.

Training as a nurse required a rigid control of the emotions, and it took several seconds before she was able to let her grief spill from behind the barrier she had erected.

'One of my favourite patients . . . someone I had a great fondness and respect for . . . passed away this

morning.' Sherry started haltingly, but her voice grew
stronger as she went on to tell Rollo about old Mr
Peterson who had spent so many months in hospital
fighting bravely against a disease which was spreading
throughout his body. She had become attached to the old
man, and his wisdom and understanding had endeared
him to her in a way that made it difficult for her to accept
that he was no longer there. 'I know I shouldn't let it
affect me in this way, but Eddie Peterson was ...
someone special,' she concluded her sad tale.

Rollo van Cleef did not say anything, but simply
tightened his fingers about hers briefly to indicate that he
understood how she felt, and that strange comforting
warmth flowed through her again. It had been a relief to
talk, and it was incredible that she could have done so to
someone she knew absolutely nothing about.

'I think it's time *you* told me something about
yourself,' Sherry prompted, sliding her hand from
beneath his. The only thing she knew about Rollo van
Cleef was that he and Jonathan had been at university
together, and that made it comparatively easy for her to
guess his age to be somewhere in the region of thirty-
three, but other than that she knew very little about this
man with the rugged good looks. 'What do you do when
you're not buying a girl coffee and letting her ramble on
about her woes?'

His eyelids descended a fraction to give his features a
lazy, rather bored expression, but she had begun to
suspect that behind those heavy-lidded eyes there lurked
a razor-sharp mind.

'I'm a scientist.'

'How very interesting!'

'It can be quite a dreary job,' he contradicted her, 'and
scientists are often considered rather dull company.'

'I don't believe that.'

'Don't you?' Rollo smiled twistedly, and her cheeks
flamed with embarrassment when their glances met and
held for breathless seconds until the sound of someone's

laughter broke the spell.

She dragged her eyes from his to drink her coffee, but she was intensely aware of the man seated opposite her, and she was even more aware of the fatal magnetism he seemed to exude. They talked while they drank their coffee, their conversation light and impersonal, and all too soon it was time to leave. It was a beautiful night, and Sherry was strangely reluctant to let it end when they stepped out into the street and stood for a moment beneath the flashing neon sign.

'Are you on a visit to Cape Town, or do you live here?' she inadvertently found herself asking him again when her curiosity got the better of her.

'I live here,' came the abrupt reply as they walked slowly in the direction of her flat.

His answer was not very informative, and she was suddenly nervous and tense when she glanced up at him. 'I'm sorry if it seems as if I'm prying,' she apologised.

'It's a warm night, and the moon is full.' He changed the subject with a gleam of mockery in his eyes as if he sensed her slight withdrawal. 'A perfect night for a stroll on the beach, wouldn't you say?'

'Perfect,' she heard herself agreeing despite the warnings flashing through her mind, and his hand was beneath her elbow, guiding her across the street before she could think up an excuse not to accompany him.

The Clifton beach was not entirely deserted. A small group of people had decided to take a midnight dip in the cold Indian Ocean, but Rollo drew Sherry in the opposite direction. She could taste the tangy sea air on her lips, and she took off her silver sandals to feel the cool, soft sand beneath her stockinged feet. She had never before walked on a beach after sunset, let alone at one o'clock in the morning, but it felt heavenly, and the peace and quiet was like balm after the long, hectic, and disturbing day. She could see and hear the waves breaking on the shore, but it was a pleasant rather than a jarring sound.

Rollo was walking beside her, and his hand beneath

her elbow was relaxed, but firm. She felt his eyes on her, willing her to look at him, but she dared not. Her nerve ends started to quiver until they had tightened into a knot at the pit of her stomach, and somewhere deep inside her there was something which was demanding a release from the chains which held it in bondage. She knew he felt the same; she sensed it in his touch as if their thoughts and feelings had become linked in some strange way, but those warning signals still flared somewhere in the back of her mind. She was hovering on the brink of a discovery, but a part of her continued to remind her of the danger involved.

'Do you live far from here?' Rollo questioned her, his voice deep and soft as the night.

'I have a flat in that tall building across the street.' She gestured vaguely with the hand that held her sandals.

'You must spend most of your free time on the beach.'

'Not really.' She had an odd feeling that their mundane conversation was a cover for something more intense, and she felt it so strongly that her heart thudded heavily against her ribs. 'There's too much to do when I'm off duty, but I do come down occasionally for a swim in the summer.'

Did that breathless, husky voice belong to her? she wondered frantically. Red lights were flashing madly in her brain. *Run before it's too late!* She wanted to obey, but Rollo's hands were on her shoulders. He turned her to face him in the moonlit darkness, and a trembling warmth surged through her. Something was happening between them, something she could not escape, and quite suddenly she knew that she did not want to escape from it.

'Sherry . . .' His hands caressed her shoulders through the thin wrap, and a thousand little nerves seemed to come alive to his touch. 'There's a certain magic in the air tonight. I don't know what it is, but I feel as if I can almost reach out and touch it.'

It would be so easy to deny it, but her conscience

warned against subterfuge. 'I—I can feel it, too.'

His eyes roamed her face to linger eventually on her quivering lips. She felt herself teetering on the brink, every nerve stretched towards something which was as yet unknown to her, and a tremor of expectancy raced through her body when she looked up into his glittering eyes.

'You're beautiful, Sherry.' His voice caressed her, and his fingers gently brushed aside a strand of hair which the playful breeze had blown across her mouth.

She caught a final glimpse of the starlit sky before he lowered his head and brushed her eyelids shut with his lips. This had to be a dream. It was the only explanation she could find for this delightful, floating sensation she was experiencing. His warm, firm mouth settled on hers at last, and the final particle of her orderly life suddenly crumbled about her. His kisses were light and explorative, seeking rather than demanding, but she was becoming aware of a growing, sensual urgency which he kept severely leashed. Sherry admired him for the control he exercised when she felt her own control slipping rapidly, and she was conscious of alien emotions clamouring for an outlet when his hands slid down her back to draw her closer to the hard length of his body.

A breath of sanity was beginning to invade this dazzling, crazy world she had drifted into. Never in her twenty-three years had she allowed her mind to be swamped like this. Men had been sadly disappointed in the past when they had expected a physical reward for an evening out, yet here she was kissing Rollo van Cleef after only a few brief hours of having met him, and she was actually *enjoying* it.

Her heart was beating so fast that she could scarcely breathe when she dragged her lips from his and leaned back against his strong supporting arms. 'Rollo, we—we hardly know each other.'

Her protest sounded hollow and unconvincing while everything within her demanded that he kiss her again

... and again.

'Time is irrelevant,' Rollo insisted softly, his glance holding hers as he released her to slide her flimsy wrap off her shoulders, and it fell to the sand where she had dropped her sandals and bag some minutes earlier. 'Tomorrow the world could go up in flames, and then we might find ourselves regretting that we never savoured these few precious moments,' he argued.

'How—how terribly fatalistic you sound!' Her laugh was shaky, and a melting sensation was invading her body when his hands circled her slender waist.

'Life is like that. We're here today and gone tomorrow, and there's so much sadness in the world that when a little happiness comes our way we ought to grasp it with both hands, even if it's only for a few brief moments.'

A flicker of fear darted through her. 'Eddie Peterson once told me something similar to that.'

'And I bet you laughed at him,' Rollo added gravely.

'I did,' she confessed in a hushed voice. 'But I'm not laughing now.'

This was a golden moment; a moment she could not allow to slip through her fingers. This was *now*, and tomorrow would take care of itself, she was thinking quite uncharacteristically, and then she was losing herself in Rollo's arms. Her lips parted beneath the sensual pressure of his mouth, and he no longer attempted to hide his desire for her as he ground his hips into hers. Intensely primitive emotions seared through her as she clung to his wide shoulders. Her trembling legs gave way beneath her, and he followed her down on to the cool white sand, his hands cradling her against him so that she lay with her head resting in the crook of his arm.

Nothing existed beyond this moment, and the roar of the sea seemed to grow louder in her ears when Rollo trailed fiery kisses down along the column of her throat and across one satiny smooth shoulder. She felt elated, as if she was being lifted beyond herself, and she could no longer ignore that deep sense of belonging which was beginning to manifest itself in her.

Rollo's body tensed against hers. One hand strayed in a light caress across the curve of her breast, then he released her and drew her up on to her feet with him.

'I'm afraid,' she whispered jerkily, trembling so much that she had to cling to him to steady herself. 'It frightens me that I can feel this way about someone I scarcely know.'

'Don't be afraid, Sherry,' he murmured, his hands framing her flushed face. 'There's nothing to be afraid of.'

His lips brushed against hers in a painfully sweet caress, then he picked up her bag and her sandals and shook the sand out of her wrap. He draped it about her shoulders, and his arm was strong and firm about her waist as they continued to walk across the now deserted beach. He steadied her when they reached the promenade so that she could put on her sandals, then they walked across the street towards the building where she lived.

Sherry felt lightheaded, as if she had had too much to drink. This could not be happening to her. She had to be dreaming. But that hard male body against her side was very real, and her lips still tingled with the memory of his kisses. She would never have believed that anything like this could happen to her. One read about it in books, and laughed about it in cynical disbelief, but suddenly she was experiencing it in reality. She had fallen madly and hopelessly in love, and the man she loved was not a stranger to her. There had been that sense of recognition when she had first seen him, and she knew now that he was the one she had subconsciously been waiting for. Rollo did not have to say anything, she knew he felt the same, and they entered the red brick building in silence and climbed the steps up to her flat on the first floor.

'It's been a memorable evening, and I shall never forget it,' he said when they stood outside her door.

'I shan't forget it either.'

He lowered his dark head and set his lips on hers in a

lingering kiss that once again activated those fiery tremors inside her. She wanted to press her body closer to his, she wanted the strength of his arms about her, but he ended the kiss abruptly, and brushed his fingers lightly against her cheek.

'*Vaarwel, liewe meisie,*' he said softly when he had taken her key from her shaky fingers to unlock her door, and the shock of his words was like a dash of sobering, icy water in the face.

'Why are you saying goodbye as if we'll never see each other again?' she demanded with a frantic urgency in her voice which she could not disguise when he would have walked away from her, and he turned to look at her with his brilliant, but shuttered eyes.

'It would be better for both of us if we never saw each other again,' he said in a strangely clipped voice. 'Believe me, Sherry.'

It felt as if the earth had suddenly been hacked away beneath her feet, and she was left to plunge into a well of confusion as she stood there watching Rollo van Cleef walk away from her. She wanted to call him back. She wanted to insist on an explanation. But no sound passed her lips, and her limbs simply refused to carry out the instructions being fired from her brain.

Her dream had become a nightmare. How dare he walk into her life, steal her heart, and then calmly walk away from her again! They belonged together, she knew it and felt it in every fibre of her being. What was more, he had felt it as well. It had been a magical night, and he had said so himself. Now the magic of it lay shattered like fine crystal at her feet.

CHAPTER TWO

THE smell of disinfectant hovered in the air in the hospital corridor, and Sherry was thrust back to reality after spending the long hours of the night on a confused and bewildered plane where nothing made sense.

'I feel dreadful!' groaned Brenda as they walked briskly towards their respective wards. 'I didn't get to bed until four this morning, and I had to be up again at six. My head's throbbing, and my insides feel as if I've had an abdominal op!'

Sherry's grey eyes mirrored instant concern when she glanced at her friend. 'You'll have to take better care of yourself in future,' she warned. 'Wild parties and pregnancy don't go well together.'

'Perhaps you're right,' Brenda agreed solemnly when they reached the men's ward where Sherry was on duty, and only then did she study Sherry more closely. 'You know, you don't look so good yourself.'

'I have a bit of a headache,' said Sherry, explaining away the ravages caused by her inability to sleep.

'Hey, I've just remembered!' Brenda exclaimed curiously. 'What happened between you and Rollo last night?'

Sherry winced inwardly as if Brenda had stabbed a careless finger into an open wound. 'Nothing happened.'

'Oh, come off it, Sherry!' Brenda laughed in disbelief. 'You both took one look at each other, fell like a ton of bricks, and rushed off together.'

Sherry wanted to say, 'I behaved like a romantic fool', but those cynical words would not pass the lump in her throat. A tall, straight figure was approaching them from the far end of the corridor, and Sherry was almost relieved at the timely arrival of the stern-faced woman

23

who was their superior.

'Matron Naudé is coming,' she warned in a whisper.

'Oh, cripes!' yelped Brenda softly, glancing swiftly over her shoulder. 'She's never liked me, and she's sure to have something to say about my bloodshot eyes!'

Matron Naudé was beside them before Brenda had the opportunity to dart away, and her sharp glance swiftly raked the two girls from head to toe before settling on Brenda with a distinct look of disapproval on her face. 'Have you been indulging in too many late nights, Nurse Lewis?'

'As a matter of fact we did have a celebration party last night,' Brenda confessed with defiance in her eyes and a hint of sarcasm in her voice. 'I got myself married and pregnant all in one day.'

For once Matron Naudé was rendered momentarily speechless, and Brenda took this opportunity to march off with her head held high.

'Was she serious?' Matron Naudé demanded when she had recovered her composure.

'Yes . . . but it didn't happen quite in that order,' Sherry felt compelled to explain Brenda's provocative statement as she stood aside for her superior to precede her into the small duty-room. 'She got herself pregnant first, and marriage followed as a matter of course.'

'Well, I'm glad the fellow did the decent thing and married her,' Matron Naudé remarked, but the disapproval was still there in her eyes when she changed the subject abruptly. 'We have a new patient coming in later today. Please see to it that the staff prepare the bed Mr Peterson used to occupy.'

Sherry's resentment flared at the cold, unemotional reference to Eddie Peterson, but she murmured respectfully, 'Yes, Matron.'

Dark brown eyes met Sherry's with keen perception, and Matron Naudé's glance softened miraculously. 'Take my advice, Sister Jaeger—never get too involved with your patients. This may sound harsh to you, and I dare say you think of me as an object devoid of emotion, but I had my fair share of agony during my first years of nursing. You're a good nursing Sister, and you certainly have the potential for even greater things, but you're going to have to learn to erect a distancing barrier between yourself and the patients, as I have had to do.'

The sharp, brisk voice had been toned down to a murmur of sympathetic understanding, and Sherry saw for the first time behind the rigid mask which had confronted her so often during the past five years. This woman was not the callous, unfeeling creature Sherry had imagined. Beneath the surface there was a woman's heart that wept and rejoiced with her patients, and Sherry began to respect and admire this grey-haired woman for more than simply her qualifications.

'Thank you, Matron,' Sherry smiled into those dark eyes, but the mask of authority had snapped back into position.

'You'd better get your staff moving, Sister Jaeger, or we'll be running late.'

'Yes, Matron,' Sherry answered briskly, and Matron Naudé marched out of the duty-room, leaving her with a lighter heart than when she had arrived at the hospital that morning.

Sherry felt strangely enriched and enlivened when she made her usual round of the men's ward, and she could almost forget the agonising hours of soul-searching she had endured during the night.

'You're looking rather glum this morning, Mr Agnew,' she commented to one of the elderly male patients while the nurses straightened his sheets and plumped up his pillows.

'The ward is just not the same without Eddie Peterson,' he complained, sighing heavily.

'Of course it's still the same,' Sherry protested, keeping a tight rein on her own feelings while she returned his chart to the foot of his bed. 'A familiar face amongst us may be gone, but I'm still here, Nurse van Rensburg is here, and so is Nurse Walters.'

The old man looked thoughtful. 'I suppose that's true, but I miss old Eddie in the bed here next to me, and I miss our early morning chats.'

Sherry and the young nurses exchanged glances, then Sherry confronted the patient gravely. 'We all miss him, Mr Agnew, but I guess he's happy where he is, and he wouldn't want us looking glum about it.'

'You're right,' he nodded slowly after yet another thoughtful silence, then he brightened perceptibly. 'I think I'll read that newspaper now, Sister.'

She passed him the newspaper which had been left untouched on his bedside locker, and he was putting on his reading glasses to study the front page when Sherry moved on to some of the other patients while the nurses continued their ritual of straightening sheets and plumping up pillows.

The morning passed swiftly with doctors coming and going, and Sherry barely had time to sit down to a cup of tea in the duty-room. The new patient arrived: a thin, jaundiced-looking man who ignored Mr Agnew's attempts at making conversation, and promptly made himself unpopular in the ward. When it was time for Sherry's lunch break she was actually relieved to escape for a few minutes.

Brenda had secured a table for them in the hospital canteen, and Sherry joined her there with a limp tomato sandwich in one hand and a cup of tea in the other. She sat down tiredly on the upright chair, and it was sheer heaven to take the weight off her feet at last. They talked shop for a few minutes, then Brenda asked the question which Sherry had subconsciously been dreading.

'What happened last night, Sherry?'

Sherry stared at the remainder of her soggy sandwich and lost her appetite completely. There was no easy way to answer Brenda's query. What feasible explanation could she give for what had happened to her last night? She had had a dream; a wild, crazy dream in which she had met the one man who had been singled out solely for her. Perhaps she had always known that she would recognise him the moment she saw him, but then she had always had the ridiculous notion that he would feel the same way about her. For one ecstatic moment on the beach last night she had believed their meeting had meant as much to him as it did to her, but the dream had been cruelly shattered.

She shook her head in an attempt to rid herself of Rollo van Cleef's image. 'I don't know what happened,' she answered confusedly.

'What do you mean, you don't know?' demanded Brenda, and she was beginning to look as bewildered as Sherry felt.

'Well, I thought . . . I imagined . . . no, *dammit*, I was *sure*!' Sherry pressed her clenched fists against her forehead in an effort to think clearly. 'Nothing like this has ever happened to me before, and I was so convinced that Rollo felt the same as I did that I was stunned when he said goodbye and told me it would be best if we never saw each other again.'

Brenda eyed her speculatively. 'Did he make love to you?'

'Most certainly not!' Sherry exclaimed indignantly, lowering her hands abruptly to the table, and glaring at Brenda for even daring to imagine she would allow any man those unmentionable intimacies without the respectability of marriage to back it.

'In that case the man must be crazy,' Brenda decided bluntly.

'Or married,' Sherry voiced the most prominent fear which had kept her awake all night.

'Did he mention a wife?' Brenda pounced on Sherry's remark.

'No, he didn't, but it would explain why he suddenly got cold feet.' Sherry shook her head and suppressed that surge of feeling which was like a fiery pain in her breast. 'I've gone nearly out of my mind trying to find an acceptable motive for his behaviour, and I've come to the conclusion that my own feelings must have been so strong that I simply imagined something which wasn't there.'

Brenda's attractive features looked sceptical. 'You don't really believe that, do you?'

'Last night I could have sworn . . . I mean, the things he said made me believe that he felt the same, but——' She halted abruptly to swallow down the lump in her throat, and she spread out her hands in a gesture of mingled despair and defeat. 'I simply don't know what to think, or what to believe.'

The two girls stared at each other a little helplessly. They had always been able to speak quite frankly to each other about their personal problems, and quite often the solution had emerged from those discussions, but there appeared to be no solution to, or simple explanation for this very bewildering incident in Sherry's life.

'How do you feel about Rollo in the cold light of day, and after a hectic morning in the ward?' Brenda broke the brief silence between them.

Sherry considered this for a moment before she answered. 'I feel as if he was part of a strange and very beautiful dream which ended in a nightmare,' she said with unaccustomed cynicism. 'I was tired last night, and I'd had an upsetting day. I was vulnerable, and perhaps a little emotionally unstable.'

'How strange,' murmured Brenda, her smooth, alabaster forehead creased in a frown. 'When I mentioned to Jonathan that Rollo had taken you home he seemed to think you might be in danger of being persuaded to hand out more than a good night kiss at your door.'

'He made no attempt to seduce me, and it's futile to continue this discussion because we would simply argue in circles without coming up with the right explanation,' Sherry sighed irritably. 'Last night is perhaps best forgotten.'

'The problem is *you're* not going to forget it that easily.'

Only Brenda could have put her finger so accurately on the very root of the problem, and Sherry winced inwardly as she pushed back her chair and got wearily to her feet. 'I have to get back on duty.'

'So do I,' Brenda announced with a grimace, getting up and following Sherry from the canteen. 'See you later.'

Rollo van Cleef's name was not mentioned again during the next few days, and Sherry was beginning to think she was recovering from the experience when she arrived home late one afternoon to find a note had been pushed under her door. She picked it up, and unfolded the small sheet of paper. The bold handwriting was unfamiliar, but the words leapt out at her, striking known chords, and quickening her pulse while she read the message twice for credibility.

Meet me in the coffee bar at seven-thirty this evening if you're free. R.

Her hand was shaking, and a million thoughts seemed to dart through her mind simultaneously until she felt herself reeling mentally. Rollo had said *goodbye*, and he had done so most emphatically. It had left her bewildered after the precious hour or two they had spent together and, when she dared to think about it, it still left her incapable of finding a reasonable explanation for his strange behaviour. Why, after four days had elapsed, was he asking her to meet him again?

A dreadful suspicion took shape in her mind, and she knew she would have no peace until she had had it confirmed, or denied. She crossed the room and lifted the telephone receiver to punch out the required number. She could hear it ringing at the other end, and moments later Brenda's voice answered.

'Have you, or Jonathan perhaps, spoken to Rollo van Cleef since the night of your party?' Sherry asked quickly before she lost her nerve.

'No, we haven't,' Brenda assured her, the surprise in her voice giving truth to her statement. 'Why do you ask?'

'I just wondered,' Sherry replied evasively, ashamed of herself for thinking Brenda might have intervened on her behalf. 'There was a note under my door when I arrived home a few minutes ago, and he wants me to meet him in the coffee bar down the street at seven-thirty.'

'Are you going?'

Brenda's query startled Sherry into giving the matter a moment of serious thought. Should she go, or should she stay away? It had taken four days to overcome, to some extent, that first traumatic meeting with Rollo. Could she risk being hurt and confused all over again? And how would she feel afterwards if she ignored his request?

'My common sense warns me to stay away,' she said at length.

'Has your common sense also warned you of the great time you will have regretting it if you don't go?' Brenda cruelly underlined Sherry's own thoughts.

'Oh, lord, Brenda, do you think I don't know that?'

'Well then, what are you going to do about it?'

Sherry had never been one to make snap decisions. When a personal crisis occurred and a decision was required, she preferred to give the matter a reasonable amount of thought. Once a decision was made she never went back on it, and she never bewailed the fact if she had made a mistake.

'What *are* you going to do?' Brenda insisted impatiently, and Sherry, for the first time in her life, made a split-second decision.

'I'm going!' she said, but there was no joy in the thought of meeting Rollo again, only a terrible apprehension.

'Good luck,' Brenda laughed a little cynically, and Sherry felt certain that she was going to need all the luck she could get to tide her through that evening as well as the future.

A strong breeze was blowing inland across the sea that night. It whipped Sherry's hair about her face, and moulded her cotton skirt to her shapely legs. Three young men ceased their conversation to cast an admiring glance in her direction when she walked past them, but Sherry was oblivious of the attention she was receiving. Ahead of her the neon sign flickered above the entrance to the coffee bar and, if she was going to change her mind about seeing Rollo, then this was the time to do so. Her steps faltered briefly, but she squared her shoulders almost at the same time and walked on.

The coffee bar was crowded, and the pleasant aroma of roasted coffee beans permeated the air. Her nervous glance skipped across the room and settled finally on the man who had risen from his chair at the far end of the room. Their eyes met, and her thudding heart missed an uncomfortable beat before it raced on madly. She walked towards him, making her way slowly between the tables, and unaware of the people seated around them. For Sherry there was only one person in that coffee bar, and his presence drew her to his side like a moth being drawn helplessly and hypnotically towards a flame.

Rollo was dressed completely in black, and there was an element of danger about him which did not escape her notice. The dim, concealed lighting in the coffee bar altered his features into a ruthless mask she had not seen the first time they had met, and he pulled out a chair for Sherry before he turned from her briefly to gesture imperiously to the approaching waiter that they wanted two coffees.

'Thank you for coming, Sherry,' he said when they sat facing each other across the small square table with the checkered cloth draped over it.

She sat there staring at him, and she tried desperately to control the feelings pounding through her. She had wanted to be cool and aloof, she had wanted to be angry, but instead she found herself having to cope with a longing which could only be assuaged by his lips and arms, and she had a dreadful feeling that it showed.

'I thought you said that it would be best if we never saw each other again,' she said at length, reminding him of his parting statement after their first brief encounter, and her voice sounded horribly shaky to her own ears.

'I know what I said, and I still feel that way most strongly,' his deep, abrupt voice struck fear into her heart, 'but I had to see you again.'

Their eyes met and held, and she had a curious sensation that they were drifting into a world where no one existed save themselves, but the moment ended with the waiter placing their coffee in front of them. He put the docket face down at Rollo's elbow, and then they were alone again.

'Are you married, Rollo?' She asked the question which had been troubling her most since their last meeting. 'Is that why you didn't want us to see each other again?'

'God knows, I wish it were that simple!' he laughed harshly, and the sound jarred her nerves, then his expression softened slightly. 'No, I'm not married, and I'm not likely to be for a long time.'

Relief was a strange thing, it made her want to laugh and cry at the same time, but she did neither as her mind probed for understanding. 'Then why did you say that we shouldn't see each other again?'

'I'm going away, Sherry,' he said, his hand reaching for hers, and she responded by curling her fingers about his. 'In two weeks time I'm leading a group of scientists and marine biologists on an expedition to the Antarctic, and it wouldn't be fair of me to involve you in a relationship which has no immediate future in it.'

His touch sent unforgettable sensations spiralling through her, but there was a coldness clutching at her heart. 'How long will you be away?'

'I can't tell you that at the moment,' he answered grimly. 'It could be a year, or perhaps longer.'

Their glances met, and his deceptively lazy eyes were guarded as he withdrew his hand, leaving hers feeling oddly naked while he swallowed down a mouthful of his black, aromatic coffee.

'I don't understand,' she murmured, helping herself absently to milk and sugar, and stirring her coffee thoughtfully. 'If you're convinced that there's no future in a relationship between us, then why am I here?'

'I wanted to make it clear that I'm not in a position to enter into a relationship with you which involves a commitment,' he said harshly, meeting her grave glance. 'If you're prepared to accept that, then we could go on from there.'

Sherry did not comment on this. She drank her coffee in silence and made an attempt to sort through the facts in her mind, but nothing seemed to make sense. If he did not want a relationship that involved a commitment, then what was the true purpose of this meeting?

'What do you want of me, Rollo?' she asked at length, breaking the somewhat strained silence between them.

'I want to spend the time I have left here in Cape Town with you. I want to see you whenever you're free, but when I get on that ship it's over, and there will be no promises made between us which we might have to break.'

He was being selfish, her logical mind warned, but there was a part of her that sensed he had been driven to this, and it was the latter which determined her decision.

'I'd rather have these two weeks with you than not see you at all,' she replied with complete honesty, and regardless of how much her feelings showed.

'You're letting your heart speak for you now, and not your mind,' he warned mockingly with an uncanny insight into the turmoil that raged inside her, but she also realised he was well aware of the unfairness of his request, and that counted in his favour.

'My mind tells me to walk out of this coffee bar and out of your life,' she laughed shakily, but her laughter was cut short when tears began to choke her.

'I shan't blame you if you choose to do that,' Rollo assured her quietly, his hand seeking hers again, and her fingers instinctively gripped his as if she was afraid that *he* might be the one to walk out of the coffee bar.

'Sometimes the heart is wiser than the mind,' she argued with herself more than with him. 'How can one be sure?'

'The heart is the most fickle instrument in the human body,' he warned cynically. 'If you think with your heart, then you're gambling with your life, so I suggest you leave your heart out of it when you make this decision.'

A shiver of fear rippled through her which she could not suppress. If he was trying to erect a wall between them, then she was not going to allow it, and quite suddenly she could not bear to continue sitting there with the table between them.

'Do we have to sit here in this crowded coffee bar?' she asked, and his blue eyes glittered with mocking laughter.

'We could go for a walk on the beach.'

'Or we could go to my flat,' she suggested, a warmth rising from her throat into her face at the memory of what had happened that night they had gone for a walk on the beach.

'I have a better idea,' Rollo said abruptly, releasing her hand and getting up. 'Let's go for a drive.'

Sherry rose from her chair, and for a brief moment they stood facing each other. He was so close that she could smell the scent of his masculine cologne, and her glance took in the width of his shoulders beneath his black leather jacket before lifting higher to his face. Their eyes met and held for a fraction of a second, but it was enough to make her tremble as if he had actually touched her.

They walked out of the coffee bar and turned left a few paces towards the white Rover Sports. Rollo unlocked the door and helped her into the front seat with its brown sheepskin upholstery before he walked round to his side of the car, and got in behind the wheel. She snapped the safety belt into position and wondered for a moment if she had made the right decision, but she forgot about her uncertainty the next instant when the powerful engine sprang alive, and the car shot away from the kerb.

Rollo drove fast, but within the speed limit, and a thousand questions suddenly crowded her mind which she knew could not be voiced. He was driving past Bantry Bay towards Sea Point, and he broke the silence only once to tell her that he was taking her to his favourite spot in Cape Town. She did not question him, but when they drove through Cape Town's city centre she began to suspect that he was taking her up on to Signal Hill.

She was right. The Rover sped along Kloof Nek Road and finally turned off on to the road that led up to Signal Hill. There were no other cars up there on that night to admire the spectacular view of the city lights, and an almost therapeutic silence settled about them when Rollo parked the car and switched off the engine.

'I don't think I'll ever get tired of this view by night,' his deep, velvety voice blended with the starlit darkness, and he undid his safety belt before turning slightly in his seat to face her. 'Have you been here before?'

'Only twice,' she confessed, a smile plucking at her mouth when she recalled those two occasions.

'Did you come with someone special?' Rollo probed mockingly, and her smile deepened.

'The first time was when I was a child, and we came up here with some relations from the northern Cape. The second time was three years ago.' Her expression sobered in the darkness of the car as she recalled the last time she had sat up there on that hill with a man. 'A friend of my brother's arrived on a visit from Australia. My brother had written and asked me to act as a guide/companion during his visit, and I agreed rather reluctantly. He wanted to see the city lights from this hill, but I soon discovered that my brother's friend was more anxious to indulge in a sexual romp.'

Rollo studied her intently. 'I gather you didn't oblige him.'

'I most certainly did not! I bit his lip, and boxed his

ears so hard they must have been ringing for hours afterwards,' she confessed. 'I never saw him again after that night, and neither has my brother mentioned him in any of his letters.' Sherry risked a glance at Rollo and realised that he was shaking with silent laughter. 'It was nothing to laugh about, I can assure you,' she rebuked him indignantly.

'I was thinking that I'd better behave myself if I don't want my ears boxed,' he explained, sobering with difficulty.

'You're different,' she argued without thinking, and her cheeks suddenly flamed when he leaned towards her.

'What makes you think I'm different?' he demanded, his expression hidden from her in the darkness as his fingers trailed down her hot cheek and stopped beneath her chin to tilt her face a fraction higher. 'I have the natural appetite and instincts of any other man, and you know as little about me as you knew about your brother's friend.'

That was true. What did she know about Rollo van Cleef other than that he was once a friend of Jonathan Hunt's?

'My instincts tell me you're not the type of man who would choose the uncomfortable interior of a car in which to seduce a woman,' she heard herself saying, and this time she felt herself blushing from the roots of her hair to the tips of her toes. What on earth had possessed her to say something like that?

She expected him to mock her, but instead he turned away from her and sat staring almost morosely through the windscreen at the brilliantly lit scene below them.

'Sherry, I had no right to imagine I could take our relationship beyond our first meeting, and I feel like a cad when I think rationally about what I asked you this evening,' he said at length, and a chill of fear shot through her.

'Are you going to walk out of my life again tonight, and leave me with no choice at all?' she asked unsteadily.

'That's what I ought to do. That's what I *know* I should do.'

'I won't let you!' she cried, her voice husky with fear. 'Sherry . . .'

'If you want a relationship with no commitments on either side, then you've got it!' she interrupted him rashly. It did not occur to her to question him on the nature of the relationship he desired, but at that moment she would recklessly have given him anything he wanted in order to spend a little more time with him.

'You haven't given the matter sufficient thought,' Rollo accused her exasperatedly, turning in his seat to face her.

He was giving her the opportunity to change her mind, but in this instance her heart overruled the warnings that flashed through her mind. 'I told you in the coffee bar that I'd rather spend the next two weeks with you than not see you at all, and I meant it.'

His hand found hers, and she welcomed the crushing firmness of his clasp. *'Liewe meisie,'* he murmured throatily, releasing her fingers to undo her safety belt. 'I hope you never regret your decision.'

'I shan't.'

She was in his arms then, and that was where she had longed to be from the moment their eyes had met in the coffee bar. He held her tightly and she clung to him as she buried her face against his shoulder to breathe in the clean male smell of him until she felt quite light-headed with his nearness. His lips brushed across her cheek in search of her mouth, and the lingering sensuality of his kisses drew a wild response from her. *Keep it cool,* she warned herself, but her body strained towards his across the gear lever space between the two seats. Her hands were beneath his jacket where she could feel the muscled warmth of his body through his shirt, and suddenly Rollo was kissing her with a passionate urgency that parted her lips for the intimate exploration of his tongue.

Sherry tried to think clearly, but her brain felt lethargic

as if a potent drug had been injected into her veins, and
all that was left was a sense of touch. His hands caressed
her slowly, their warmth arousing sensual fires, and
exquisite sensations that rippled through her body. His
fingers undid the tiny buttons down the front of her
blouse, but she was beyond caring when his fingers
brushed aside her silky bra to stroke the swell of her
breast, and his caress awakened feelings so intense that
she trembled with the force of them.

The intimacy of his touch was new to her, it was
something she had never allowed before, but with Rollo
it seemed so right that she made no attempt to stop him
when his fingers teased her nipple into a hard, aching
button. She wanted him to touch her, and fast on the
heels of this discovery came the startling knowledge that
she wanted him to touch her all over. His mouth left hers
to seek out the hardened peak of her breast, and a little
moan escaped her at the exquisite sensations surging
through her to become centred in her loins. Her hands
found their way into his shirt to stroke his hair-
roughened chest and his shoulders where his muscles
knotted together, and she was lost in the whirlpool of her
own emotions when she felt Rollo shudder against her
and bury his face for a moment in the scented hollow
between her breasts, then he released her abruptly and
turned the key in the car's ignition.

Sherry sat there feeling stunned while Rollo pulled
away with tyres spinning on the gravel. Her fingers were
shaking so much that she had difficulty in fastening the
buttons down the front of her blouse. What was wrong?
Why wasn't he talking to her? Did she do something to
anger him?

She was nervous and tense during the drive back to
Clifton, and it was only when he had unlocked the door
to her flat that she risked questioning his behaviour.

'Rollo, did I—did I do something wrong?'

'*Liewe meisie,*' he laughed unexpectedly, tapping an
admonishing finger against her cheek. 'You're so

innocent, it just isn't true.'

There was a flash of anger in the grey eyes that met his. 'If you mean inexperienced in matters concerning sex——'

'I meant *innocent* in not knowing how easily a man can be aroused,' he interrupted to correct her. 'You're a beautiful young woman, and I warned you that I'm a very normal man. I want you, and I know you want me, but I'm not going to force you into a relationship that doesn't appeal to you.'

He kissed her hard on the mouth and walked away to leave her thoughtful and a little bewildered as she entered her flat and locked the door behind her. He was not going to force her into a relationship which did not appeal to her, he had said, and she ought to have felt relieved, but instead she felt vaguely hurt and annoyed.

CHAPTER THREE

BRENDA was curious to know the details of Sherry's meeting with Rollo, but Sherry was reluctant to talk about it. Her feelings were too personal, her fears too real, and the uncertainty and confusion which confronted her was something only she could deal with. She had embarked on something which was going to leave her hurt, and possibly disillusioned. In broad daylight, and away from Rollo, she could see that she was heading towards disaster; but she felt as if she had been caught midstream in a fast flowing river, and there was nothing for her to clutch at for safety.

Rollo telephoned her at work the very next day, and his voice had the same magical effect as his presence. 'I have two tickets for the theatre this evening,' he said briefly. 'Would you like to go?'

'I'd love to,' she accepted without hesitation, and his

mocking laughter came softly over the line.

'You haven't even asked what play is on at the Nico Malan theatre.'

'It doesn't matter,' she answered with inexplicable conviction. 'Where the arts are concerned I know you have impeccable taste.'

There was a brief silence before he asked, 'How do you know so much about me without being told?'

'I guessed.' She tried to brush off something which she could not even explain to herself.

'I'll call for you at seven-thirty,' he ended the conversation abruptly, and Sherry stood frowning down at the lifeless receiver in her hand for some seconds before she lowered it on to its cradle.

'Is there something the matter, Sister Jaeger?'

Sherry looked up in surprise to see Matron Naudé observing her intently, and she rose respectfully behind her desk, shaking her head slowly. 'I was just wondering . . .'

'Wondering *what*?' the woman prompted impatiently, gesturing Sherry back into her chair and seating herself so that they faced each other across the desk.

'Is it possible to meet someone and to feel you've known that person all your life?' Sherry questioned Matron Naudé gravely.

'It has happened before, I believe.'

'To the extent that one is actually aware of certain things about this person without being told?'

'That's possible too.' Matron Naudé's keen glance sharpened. 'Have you met someone who makes you feel like that?'

'Yes.'

'A man?' Matron Naudé asked with extraordinary perception, and Sherry felt herself blushing.

'Yes,' she confessed with her usual honesty.

'If I could give you some advice, then I would suggest you don't allow yourself to be influenced by this,' Matron Naudé warned with a gravity that bordered on concern.

'I wouldn't want to see you hurt, which you might well be, and you can put that down to an extra-sensory perception of my own.'

Matron abruptly altered the conversation to matters of greater urgency, but for the rest of that day Sherry felt deeply disturbed, and even more so since her own fears had been voiced by Matron Naudé. She knew she was going to be hurt, and yet she could not halt her progress along the path towards her eventual unhappiness.

She felt tense and unsure of herself that evening, but, when Rollo's hand found hers in the darkened theatre, she had come to terms with the decision she had made.

'You were very quiet during the early part of this evening,' Rollo remarked when she had made them coffee in her flat after returning from the theatre. 'Are you having doubts about the wisdom of your decision to become involved with a man like myself?'

Sherry was silent for a moment. He had discarded his evening jacket and he had loosened his tie, but it was not his general appearance that captured and held her attention. She sensed that behind his mockery there lurked an attitude of defeat and a certain amount of fear, but most of all there was the feeling that he, too, was heading towards something he could not avoid. Compassion came from nowhere to flood her heart, and she put down her cup to join him on her bright, floral sofa.

'I'm not going to deny that I've had doubts about my decision,' she confessed with honesty, 'but I want you to know that I don't regret it now. You have your job to do, you accepted the leadership of this expedition to the Antarctic, and I accept the fact that we'll have only a short time together.'

He stared at her for some time before he pulled her into his arms, and there was something so desperate in the way he kissed and caressed her that she had the strongest desire to cry, but she somehow held her tears in check.

'Did you know that Rollo is a professor in science and

that he's leaving in two weeks' time for the Antarctic?'
Brenda pounced on Sherry the very next day when they
were having lunch in the canteen. 'Did he tell you that
he's going to be away for a year or more?'

So Rollo was a *professor*, was he? This was something
she had not known, but to Brenda she said, 'Yes, he told
me.'

'Take my advice, Sherry, and stay away from him.'
Brenda pushed her plate aside and poured their tea. 'The
man's not going to commit himself in any way almost on
the eve of his departure, and a year, and heaven knows
how many months, is a long time to wait for something
that might never happen.'

That was true. Sherry could not deny that to herself,
and neither had Rollo attempted to hide from her the fact
that he was not in a position to commit himself, but it
angered her to have Brenda underlining her own fears.

'Thanks for the advice,' she said coldly, 'but I think
I'm old enough to decide for myself what I want to do.'

'Sherry, I'm sorry,' Brenda apologised at once, her
hazel eyes shadowed with concern. 'I'm so afraid you
might be hurt.'

'I can take care of myself,' Sherry assured her friend,
but she could not eliminate her own anxiety. There *was*
no future in this relationship with Rollo, and yet she did
not want to end it. In the depths of her heart there was a
flicker of hope that refused to be quelled, and she clung to
it rather desperately. She glanced at her watch and
hastily swallowed down the last of her tea. 'Come on,' she
smiled at Brenda. 'It's time we got back to work.'

Sherry stood by her decision, but during the days that
followed she found herself having to cope with the
frustrations that accompanied their unsatisfactory relationship. She loved him, and every meeting served to
strengthen that knowledge. She loved the way his mouth
curved in that faintly mocking smile, and she loved the
way he arranged little surprises for her, but most of all
she loved him for his gentleness and his restraint when

passion drove them into each other's arms. His touch lit a
fire in her, and his kisses awakened an aching need that
made her realise at last how foolish she had been to
condemn Brenda. She knew now what it meant to love
someone so desperately that all one could think of was
the desire to belong to that person entirely, and it was
sheer hell trying to cling to her beliefs while her body
craved fulfilment. She wanted him, and she could have
him. It was as simple as that, but a part of her still shied
away from the thought.

They spent every moment of her free time together. He
took her up on to Table Mountain on her afternoon off
and told her how he had climbed it during his student
days. They had tea in the restaurant built solely of stones,
and he seemed reluctant to leave when it was time to take
the cable car down to the cable station. He mocked her
when she insisted on buying the photograph taken of
them when they had ascended the mountain, but she had
a feeling that it pleased him to know that she wanted
something to remember him by.

The two weeks passed much too soon, and it ended
with a crucial encounter which affected Sherry's future
drastically. Rollo had arranged that they would take a
drive around the peninsula on the Sunday afternoon, but
he did not arrive at the stipulated time to fetch her. She
was annoyed at first, thinking he had changed his mind
without letting her know, but as the afternoon progressed
she became convinced that something was wrong. She
knew where he lived, they had driven past his gabled
home on two occasions, and a gnawing fear finally drove
her out of her flat on that cool, cloudy afternoon.

She sped towards Constantia in her Mini as if
something was chasing her, but when she reached the
turn-off to his home she stopped her car and paused to
consider the situation. What if he did not want to see
her? And, worse still, what if he had left already without
bothering to say goodbye?

She put her foot down on the accelerator and the Mini

raced up the long drive to the house. A coloured man was loosening up the soil among the shrubs in the vast garden with its well-kept lawn, but Sherry barely noticed her surroundings when she got out of the Mini and climbed the few steps to the heavy oak door. She lifted the brass knocker and brought it down sharply twice. She waited, her heart suddenly beating in her mouth, and then the door was opened by a coloured woman in a blue overall and white apron.

'Is Professor van Cleef at home?' Sherry asked at once.

'The professor is not well, and he won't see anyone,' came the reply that stunned Sherry momentarily. She had been right after all.

'I'm a nurse, perhaps I can help him.' She spoke with a briskness she had often heard in Matron Naudé's voice. 'Which is the way to his room?'

The coloured woman hesitated, uncertain about what to do, then she said reluctantly, 'Turn left when you get upstairs, and the professor's room is at the end of the passage.'

Sherry crossed the carpeted hall and went quickly up the stairs, her hand at times gripping the intricately carved wooden balustrade. Her heart was beating in her mouth again when she took the passage to the left, but the professional side of her took command when she entered Rollo's bedroom to find him lying fully clothed on his disorderly bed. His eyes were closed, but he must have sensed her presence as she approached the bed, and his thick, dark lashes lifted to reveal angry, pain-filled eyes.

'What the hell are you doing here?' he groaned harshly.

'I realised that something was wrong when you didn't turn up for our appointment this afternoon,' she explained, seating herself gingerly on the side of the bed when her legs suddenly felt incapable of carrying her weight. 'I believe you're ill, and I thought I could help.'

'It's migraine,' he said in a clipped voice. 'I get it very

rarely, and it's nothing to worry about.'

'Have you taken something for it?' she asked, her clinical glance taking in the deep grooves along the sides of his tight mouth, and the film of perspiration on his forehead.

'Yes, I have,' he grunted irritably, rolling over and turning his back on her. 'Stop fussing, Sherry.'

He needed help and, despite his protestations, she was going to give it to him. She left his room quietly and went in search of the kitchen. The coloured woman who had met Sherry at the door earlier was helpful. She emptied an ice tray into a basin of cold water and supplied her with a small towel out of her linen cupboard.

Armed with this primitive remedy, Sherry went upstairs again. Rollo had turned over on to his back again, and his lazy-lidded eyes widened with a mixture of mockery and despair. 'Don't you ever do as you're told?'

'Mostly,' she smiled at him, despite her concern, 'but this is an exception.'

'Like hell it is!' he contradicted her harshly, but she took no notice.

She sat on the bed beside him, and soaked the towel in the iced water, then she wrung it out, and placed it against his hot forehead. He closed his eyes, obviously finding her ministrations pleasing, and she repeated this procedure several times within the next half hour before she saw his facial muscles relax.

'Feeling better?' she asked eventually when she removed the towel and dropped it into the basin for the last time.

'Much better,' he smiled faintly. 'I'll prove it to you.'

He pulled her down into his arms, and she made no attempt to avoid his mouth. His kisses were demanding, his caresses a little wild, and Sherry responded with a wildness of her own. She tugged at his shirt buttons and slid her hands across his bare chest, loving the feel of his damp, hair-roughened skin beneath her palms. Their time together was limited, and God only knew what she was going to do when he was gone.

They drew apart slowly, reluctantly, and Rollo's fingers traced the soft curve of her cheek in a playful, almost admonishing caress. She raised her hand to cover his where it lay against her cheek, and she closed her eyes to hold back the tears when she turned her lips into his palm for long disturbing seconds.

'What are we going to do?' she asked, and her voice was no more than a husky murmur. 'I think we both know that we can't just walk away from each other as if the past two weeks never happened.'

Rollo's rugged features hardened, his eyes narrowed, and she felt a coldness sliding beneath her skin when he rolled away from her, pulling the silky bedspread into further disarray as he got up off the bed and crossed the room to stand staring out of the window. 'I'm going away soon, Sherry. I can't take you with me, and I'm not asking you to wait for me.'

'Don't you want me to wait for you?'

'Sherry!' he warned without turning.

'I know,' she sighed despairingly, and with a touch of anger. 'I know I agreed to a relationship with no commitments on either side, but——'

'Then let's leave it at that,' he warned harshly, but her growing resentment would not let her heed his warning.

'I can't leave it there!' she cried hoarsely, blinking back her tears as she got to her feet to join him at the window. 'Rollo, you can't tell me that these past two weeks haven't meant something to you, and I won't believe that you can simply walk out of my life without giving me some sort of hope for the future.'

'*Dammit*, Sherry!' he exploded with a savage harshness that made her shrink away from him when he spun round to face her. 'If it's a commitment you want, then you're looking at the wrong man, and you can't say I didn't warn you about that.'

Sherry felt as if she was hovering on the edge of a dangerous precipice. She could plummet down into the hell below, or she could be drawn to safety. Whichever the outcome, her fate was in his hands. Terror spilled ill-chosen words into her mouth and gave a sharp edge to her voice when she stared up at this man with the snarling features who had suddenly become a stranger to her.

'You're making me wonder why I got myself involved in this crazy set-up in the first place, and why I should bother to see you again!'

'I'm beginning to wonder that myself!' he retaliated, and the swift, sharp sting of his words sent her over that edge into the hell she had feared.

He did not mean that! She could not, and would not, believe what he had just said, but his features remained harsh and unyielding. She waited, hoping and praying that he would take her in his arms and laugh away this incident, but nothing like that happened. He turned from her to stare out of the window as if she disgusted him, and it felt as if he had slammed a door in her face. Oh, God, it hurt! She had never dreamed it would come to this, but she knew now that it was what she had feared from the start.

It was over. Those three words seemed to echo repeatedly through her mind. Her eyes filled with stinging tears as she turned and walked out of his room and out of his house without looking back. *It was over.*

Sherry never slept that night. Her mind was bursting with those dreadful, damning words they had said to each other. *You're making me wonder why I got myself involved in this crazy set-up, in the first place, and why I should bother to see you again,* her own words stabbed her to the core, and were followed swiftly with Rollo's, *I'm beginning to wonder that myself.*

Oh, *why* had she said something so idiotic? What on earth had possessed her to slam the door in her own face?

Work was the only antidote Sherry could think of to help her cope with her misery and pain, and the following morning she flung herself into her duties with a fierceness that had Matron Naudé raise her eyebrows on several occasions. Two days later, however, Matron Naudé's eyes began to mirror concern, but Sherry was unaware of this when she was summoned into the Matron's private sanctum.

Matron Naudé closed the door to her office. This was something she did only when she was about to reprimand one of her staff, and Sherry's overworked mind leapt about frantically. What had she done wrong? Where had she defaulted?

Her hands fluttered in a smoothing action against the skirt of her white uniform, and she clenched them nervously behind her back when she realised that her superior's sharp glance had followed that unnecessary action.

'I want you to take the afternoon off,' Matron Naudé announced, seating herself behind her desk, and her expression was shuttered when Sherry's startled glance met hers.

'I don't need to have the afternoon off, Matron,' Sherry protested, every part of her rejecting the idea of going home to her silent flat where idleness would allow too much time for thought.

'For some obscure reason you've been working at an ungodly pace these past two days, and I have no desire to see you collapse in my hospital.' Matron Naudé spoke with a sharpness edged with concern. 'I'm giving you the afternoon off, and I suggest you go home and sort out whatever it is that's driving you to your own destruction.'

That was exactly what Sherry did not want. There was nothing to sort out. Everything was so absolutely final, and all she had left was the pain of knowing she had lost the only man she could ever love.

'That was an order, Sister Jaeger,' Matron Naudé said sternly when Sherry was about to object, and the look on her superior's face told Sherry that it would be unwise to argue.

'Yes, Matron,' Sherry sighed helplessly, and she

turned and walked quickly out of the Matron's office when desolate tears filled her eyes.

It was a grey, dismal day with intermittent showers. It was not at all the type of day she would have chosen to stay at home alone with her thoughts. She got into her Mini and wondered if she ought to take a drive somewhere to help pass the time, but she decided against it almost instantly, and turned the key in the Mini's ignition. She did not particularly enjoy driving about on her own, and neither did she want to visit Brenda. She knew that Brenda would want an explanation, and an explanation was the last thing Sherry was in the mood for. How could she explain that she had fallen in love with a man whom she knew virtually nothing about? How could she explain that she had chosen to become involved with a man who had stipulated that their relationship had to be one without commitment on either side? And how could she make Brenda understand why she had agreed to such a relationship when *she* did not understand it fully herself?

Sherry drove through the hospital gates and turned her car in the direction of her flat in Clifton. She had to see this through on her own, and she could not blame anyone but herself for the mess her life was in.

She spent her time cleaning out her cupboards and vigorously polishing the furniture in her flat until she could almost see her reflection in the wood. She hated doing these chores at the best of times, but she had to do something to keep herself occupied during that long, dreary afternoon. She cooked herself a meal, using a recipe that needed her undivided attention, but, when she sat down to eat it, her food became lodged in her throat as if she had swallowed a boulder. She felt like crying, but instead she whipped up an ice-cream for herself, and ate it while she sat staring at the stack of dishes that needed to be washed.

It was after eight o'clock that evening before she had cleared away everything in the kitchen to leave it tidy. A

soak in a hot, scented bath was the next item on the busy
agenda she had drawn up for herself, but it also
happened to be the last item. It was too early to go to bed,
so she took her time and washed her hair as well. The
shampoo got into her eyes and made them burn, and they
were still smarting when she eventually emerged from
the bathroom in a wide-sleeved silk robe with a towel tied
like a turban about her hair.

She sat down in front of the dressing table mirror and
stared at herself absently. Red-rimmed eyes stared back
at her with a lifeless quality in their depths, and her
shiny, scrubbed face made her look like a sixteen-year-
old instead of a woman of twenty-three. *Damn!* she
cursed silently as she unwrapped the towel about her
head, and rubbed her hair dry as much as possible before
she plugged in the hair drier. She would look and feel
better when she had done something with her hair, she
told herself, and an application of face-cream might
succeed in taking that tight feeling out of her cheeks.

Sherry studied herself in the mirror half an hour later.
Her hair was dry and she had brushed it until it shone,
but her facial muscles still felt taut despite the thin film of
cream she had applied. 'Relax!' she told herself. 'For
God's sake relax and don't allow your thoughts to act like
the devil cracking a whip behind you.'

She breathed in deeply and expelled the air slowly
between her parted lips, but that tense, chased feeling
persisted. What was she going to do? It was too early to
go to bed, and she dreaded the thought of lying awake
with nothing but her thoughts for company.

The doorbell chimed. It was not a particularly loud
sound, but it made her jump as if a shot had been fired
beside her. Her glance darted towards the alarm clock
beside her bed. Nine-thirty! Who could be calling at this
hour? The bell chimed again, agitatedly, and Sherry
came alive with a start. There was only one person . . . !

She darted out of her bedroom and ran barefoot across
the lounge to glance through the peephole in the door.

Rollo stood there: tall, dark, and grim-faced. Her heart went wild, beating like a sledge-hammer against her ribs as joy surged through her. He had not meant those dreadful words, just as she had not meant what she had said at their last meeting, and her fingers fumbled with the latch in her haste to unlock the door. She flung it open, his name on her lips, and she might have leapt into his arms if something in his manner had not warned her that this was not the right moment for a display of that nature.

'May I come in?' he asked, and she stood aside without speaking.

He stepped past her, and she locked the door securely before she led the way into her small but spotless lounge, with its gaily-coloured cushions and homely atmosphere.

'Could I make you some coffee?' she offered, suddenly nervous, and he shook his head while he took off his black leather jacket and flung it on to a chair.

'Not just yet,' he said, his penetrating glance sliding over her in a way that convinced her he was fully aware of the fact that she had nothing on underneath her robe.

'I'll get some clothes on,' she murmured hastily, turning from him to go to her room, but his fingers snaked about her wrist to spin her round until she faced him again.

'That can wait too.' His face had lost none of its grimness, and a coldness began to invade her heart and her limbs. 'I've come to say goodbye.'

'No, Rollo! Not yet ... *please!*' she cried in alarm, clutching at his arms when the room tilted dangerously about her.

'*Yes*, Sherry,' he contradicted, his hands circling her waist in a steadying grip. 'I have no choice in the matter. It was all planned long before I met you, and the ship leaves tomorrow morning at seven.'

'Oh, God!' She broke free of him to bury her white, quivering face in her hands for a moment while the terrible truth washed over her in its entirety, and her future suddenly lay stretched out in front of her like a desolate, barren wasteland. 'I wish you could take me with you, Rollo,' she whispered when she had succeeded in controlling her features sufficiently to lower her hands.

His eyes burned down into hers, probed behind her despair, and looked deep into her stubborn, disbelieving heart. This could not be happening, she was telling herself. How could life be so cruel? He was standing no more than a pace away from her; so vital, so alive, and yet so far removed from her that it felt as if a mental chasm had developed between them. She turned from him and absently took a mutilated daisy out of the glass vase. It looked withered and pathetic as she twirled it between her fingers, and she could not help but associate its appearance with the way she felt at that moment.

'I don't suppose you would write to me, would you?' she heard herself asking a futile, silly question.

'I've never been good at writing letters.'

That hint of finality in his voice frightened her, and she knew him well enough to know that she must not expect more of him. If their relationship had to be severed, then he would do it swiftly. He was going to walk out of her life, and she knew she might never see him again. An intense longing tore through her. She tried valiantly to suppress it, but she could not fight against it, and she knew then that never again would she dare to ridicule, or condemn, Brenda.

The daisy fell from her fingers when she heard Rollo move behind her, and she was terrified that he would leave before she had had the opportunity to say what was on her mind. 'Do you have to leave immediately, or can you stay a while?' she asked in a breathless rush.

'I'm free until the ship leaves at seven tomorrow.'

'Rollo, would you——' Her face was white and strained with the fierce battle going on inside of her. It was not an easy matter to go against everything she had always believed in, but she loved him desperately. She wanted him to remember her, and she prayed that he would come back to her, but habit dies hard, and several vital seconds elapsed before she found the courage to whisper, 'Will you stay with me tonight?'

A terrifying little silence followed her request, and she could not turn to face him while her colour came and went with the enormity of what she had suggested.

'Do you know what you're saying?' he questioned her at length in a voice that sounded oddly rasping. 'If I didn't know you so well I would think that you're asking me to stay and make love to you.'

This was a heaven-sent opportunity to change her mind if she wished to do so. She could laugh it off, and pretend that she had meant it innocently, but despair and longing would not let her do so.

'If I'm never going to see you again . . .' She swallowed convulsively and fought against the tears that threatened to choke her. 'If this has to be goodbye for ever, then I'm asking you to give me this one night with you and . . . I *am* asking you to stay and make love to me.'

'Sherry . . .' His hands bit into her shoulders, burning her through the thin, silky material that covered her otherwise naked body as he turned her to face him, and his eyes were filled with his own private torment as they blazed down into hers. 'You'll regret this in the morning,' he warned. 'Have you thought of that?'

'I don't want to think about tomorrow morning!' she cried, and she could no longer stem the flow of tears as she clutched at him blindly. 'This is tonight, and I'm asking you to stay with me.'

Don't refuse me, she pleaded silently, her body trembling beneath his hands. *Now that I've come this far, please don't refuse me!*

Rollo's hands slid beneath her hair to frame her face, his thumbs brushing away the tears on her cheeks and catching the drops that rolled off her lashes. 'Don't think for one moment that I don't want to stay with you. I've wanted this from the first instant I set eyes on you, but——'

'I love you,' she interrupted him, the long withheld confession coming on a sob of despair, and she heard him draw his breath in sharply.

'Sherry, *liewe meisie*,' he groaned, pulling her roughly against him so that her face was buried against his chest. 'Life is difficult enough, don't you think?'

She slid her hands up across his broad back, and her hips swayed invitingly against him. 'Are you going to refuse me?'

For one terrible moment nothing happened, then she felt the taut heat of his desire, and there was a fierce hunger in the bruising passion of his mouth on hers. His hands moulded her to the muscled length of his body, leaving her in no doubt that he wanted her as much as she wanted him, and she shut her mind finally to that now faint little voice that warned against what she was about to do.

Sherry slipped her arms about Rollo's neck when he lifted her high in his arms and carried her into the bedroom. Her robe had parted in the process to expose one silky thigh, but she did not care. His glance lingered in a caress on her delicate features, then it ventured lower to where the opening of her robe had shifted to reveal the scented valley between her breasts. Their lips met in a lingering, sensual kiss that lit an unmistakable fire between them, and now there was not a single doubt left in her mind.

Rollo lowered her feet to the floor, and there was a measure of restraint in his manner when he eased his mouth from hers. 'Sherry, I feel like a cad. Are you sure this is what you want?'

'I'm sure,' she murmured, and her eyes never left his as she proceeded to convince him.

She raised her hands to the belt of her robe, untying it slowly, and just as slowly she slid the robe off her shoulders until it lay on the floor at her feet. A flame leapt in Rollo's eyes, and her pulse quickened when his fiery glance roamed the length of her naked body.

'My God, you're beautiful!' he breathed hoarsely, his eyes lingering now on her firm young breasts and the curve of her hips and shapely thighs, then he began to discard his own clothes with quick, jerky movements.

His body was tanned, the muscles rippling across his wide chest and along his arms. His lean hips were pale where the sun had not touched him, and his legs were long and muscular. If a man could be beautiful, then Sherry found Rollo beautiful at that moment. There was not an ounce of superfluous flesh on his body as he stood there facing her like a tall Apollo, and loving him as much as she did made this moment sacred. There was no shame in what they were going to do, and no embarrassment.

She stepped up to him and slipped her arms about his lean waist. The abrasiveness of his chest hair against her breasts excited her, and her body was soft and yielding against the hard warmth of his. She raised her lips to his, and he parted them beneath his own, his tongue exploring the sensitive sweetness within while his fingers trailed a seductive path down the hollow of her back to awaken a thousand little nerves to the pleasure of his touch. There was only one agonising thought in her mind at that moment. This one night might well have to last her for the rest of her life, and she wanted to savour every precious moment of this togetherness.

She was lifted in his arms and lowered gently on to the bed. He leaned over her for a moment, his blue eyes aflame with desire as they devoured her, then he lowered himself on to the bed beside her and aroused her with skilful, intimate little caresses that acquainted her with sensations so intensely pleasurable that an aching fire spread into the lower half of her body.

Nothing else mattered beyond this moment. A delightful mist clouded her mind and left no room for thought. His fingers caressed her inner thighs, tormenting her as they slowly worked their way up towards the heated core of her womanhood, and when, at last, his fingers stroked her with a deep, gentle intimacy, she was sent spiralling to mad heights where she was only vaguely aware of her own ragged voice pleading with him to take her.

He parted her thighs, raising his body above her, and no one could have prepared Sherry for the reality of this moment. There was a slight stab of pain as he entered her, but it was swiftly doused as his thrusting body aroused sensations so piercingly sweet that she clung to Rollo in wild abandon, begging him never to stop. He laughed throatily, a triumphant, conquering laugh that seemed to excite her more, and she was driven to a peak where it felt as if she was going to die with love for him if something did not happen soon. She had long since lost control of her mind and her body as she writhed beneath him. Her body was craving that something elusive which she, as yet, had no knowledge of, and when at last she was delivered from that pleasurable, aching tautness which had held her prisoner, she knew the true meaning of fulfilment. The pleasure of it washed over her repeatedly, and she went limp beneath the shuddering weight of Rollo's body. He had made her a woman in every sense of the word, and he had filled her soul with a radiance that had lifted her beyond the realms of this earth into another world.

Reality threatened her happiness when he lifted himself away from her, and it brought renewed despair at the knowledge that these moments could not last for ever. Rollo held her in his arms, and she turned her face into his shoulder. She did not want to think of tomorrow. It cast a shadow over this brief moment of happiness, and she could not bear anything to mar these hours with this man she loved so desperately.

CHAPTER FOUR

SHERRY had lulled her mind into a false state of euphoria from which she did not want to emerge, but Rollo's deep, vibrant voice brought her sharply back to reality.

'What thoughts, I wonder, are going through this pretty head of yours?' he said, his fingers gently brushing her hair away from her flushed face, and Sherry swiftly sorted through the multitude of thoughts she had harboured in her mind to give him a truthful answer.

'I was thinking I shall remember this night for as long as I live,' she sighed, raising herself on to one elbow to look down at him with a dreamy expression still lingering in her grey eyes. 'What were you thinking?'

His smile became tainted with a hint of annoyance. 'I was thinking we were both crazy enough not to consider the possibility that you might become pregnant.'

It was a sobering thought, but it was not one which had not crossed her mind. 'That's a chance I was willing to take when I asked you to stay.'

'What will you do if you——'

She silenced him with her fingers against his lips. 'I'll cross that bridge when I come to it . . . *if* I come to it.'

His lips moved against her fingers, then he took her hand in his and nibbled at the tip of each finger. Little shivers of erotic pleasure raced through her, and she snuggled down beside him and buried her face against his shoulder once again. This was something so new to her, this swift and trembling arousal of feelings she had not known she possessed, and she was completely overawed by it.

They both lapsed into a silence which lasted for some time. Sherry was afraid to speak, afraid to put into words the thoughts and fears that mingled into something that made her cling to every second in the hope of stretching it into an eternity. This night would end, they both knew it, but neither of them wanted to talk about it. There was, after all, no need for words when they could touch and explore each other as lovers all over the world must do, but their stroking hands spoke a language that held no promise for the future.

Rollo pulled her against him suddenly, his lips and hands demanding and receiving an instant response and, as passion flared between them, they made love for the second time that night with an urgency that shattered every last barrier between them. They held nothing back as mind, body and soul became fused in the raging torrent of emotion that swept over them, and it left them both exhausted when they finally drew apart.

Sherry's descent from that ecstatic sphere was slow and wholly pleasant as she nestled against Rollo's broad chest. His arms held her loosely, but firmly, and it was a long time before her breathing was sufficiently normal to allow her to speak.

'Was it very brazen of me to ask you to stay and make love to me?' she asked, desperately needing his reassurance.

'You couldn't be brazen even if you tried, and I shall never forget that you entrusted yourself to me tonight,' he murmured, brushing his lips in a tender caress against her temple, and his words brought reality rushing back with a force that gave her a taste of the cold, desolate world she would have to face in the morning.

She turned her head so that she could see his face, and she lazily traced the contours of his ruggedly handsome features with the tips of her fingers. It was not enough to look at him, she had to touch him. She was going to be brave, there were going to be no tears, but the faintly mocking smile that curved Rollo's mouth was her undoing. It was as if he had read her thoughts, and helpless tears filled her eyes.

'Oh, Rollo, how am I going to——'

He silenced her with a hard, satisfying kiss, and he went on kissing her until her tense body relaxed against his.

'Let's not make it more difficult than it already is,' he warned gravely and, stretching out his arm, he switched off the bedside light to plunge the room into darkness. 'Go to sleep, Sherry, and dream of me as I shall dream of you.'

Sherry did not answer him. It was better to let him think that she had agreed to his suggestion, but this was one night when she did not want to sleep. She wanted to lie in his arms and savour his nearness through the night, for the future would be lonely and empty for her without him. She stared into the darkness, the hard warmth of his body warming her outwardly, but it did not reach that coldness deep inside her. The bedside clock ticked away each precious second with a swiftness that made her want to scream abuse at it, and it was not long before Rollo's deep, even breathing told her that he was asleep.

How could he sleep at a time like this? Didn't he care that tomorrow would herald a parting which would bring her world crashing about her ears?

She slid her hand in a gentle caress across his chest and felt the roughness of hair against her fingers and her palm. Beneath her ear she could hear the slow, steady beat of his heart, but twice that night she had felt it drumming at a fierce pace against her breast. She did not regret what she had done, she would never regret it while there was still the irrepressible hope that Rollo might one day come back to her. A year, after all, was not too long to wait, but, until then, this one night would have to sustain her through the weeks and months to come.

Despite her determination to stay awake, Sherry drifted into a deep and dreamless sleep from which she did not awaken until the alarm rang loudly on the bedside cupboard. She stretched out a hand to silence it and yawned sleepily behind her hand. She felt lazy, and extremely unwilling to stir between the sheets, but the next instant a puzzled frown creased her brow. Why had she gone to bed without wearing her nightgown?

The answer came in one sickening rush of agonising misery, and she sat up with a jerk, her eyes darting wildly about the room. Rollo's clothes were not on the chair where he had flung them the night before. He had left while she was asleep, and he had not said goodbye.

Why didn't he wake me! her heart cried out in silent despair. She lifted the pillow where his head had lain, and buried her face in it, but as she did so her glance caught sight of a piece of paper fluttering across the bed. She flung the pillow aside and snatched up the note. A cry of anguish passed her lips as Rollo's bold handwriting leapt out at her, and it was several seconds before she could control herself sufficiently to read what he had written.

Sherry, sweet girl, you were sleeping like a baby, and I didn't have the heart to wake you. Saying goodbye is never easy, and I would prefer to remember you with no tears in your eyes.

If I'm any good at guessing your thoughts, then I imagine you have some crazy idea about waiting for me. Forget it, Sherry. Many things can happen in a year, or possibly more. People change, feelings change, so if you meet someone who could make you happy, then you should marry him rather than waste your time waiting for a man who took so much from you without giving anything in return.

I shall never forget your loving generosity last night. Rollo.

There was something in his letter that troubled her, but she could not define it at first, and she read the letter through twice before she discovered what it was. He did not want her to wait for him because he had taken so much from her without giving anything in return.

It was this that led to the most humiliating discovery of all. She had told him that she loved him; she had stripped herself naked body and soul for him, and not once had he said that he loved *her*. She had believed that he cared, and his murmured endearments last night had convinced her, but she realised now that *love* had never been mentioned other than by herself.

What did you expect? she asked herself, anguished tears filling her eyes. Didn't he make it quite clear from the start that it would have to be a relationship with no commitments on either side? He never asked you to love him, did he?

Sherry curled herself up into a ball of misery on the bed. Rollo was gone, it was possible that she would never see him again, and the facts were beginning to shout the truth at her which she could not ignore. She wept tears of anger and self-pity for which she despised herself afterwards, but that was the last time she allowed herself the luxury of tears.

Sherry's work was her only form of survival, and she flung herself into it with a determination and perspicacity she had never displayed before. She tried not to think about Rollo, but it was not an easy task to forget someone who had become so much a part of her life in such a short space of time. When Brenda questioned her about Rollo, Sherry said simply, 'It's over', but Brenda's curiosity was far from being satisfied.

Six weeks later Brenda left the hospital when the growing evidence of her pregnancy finally forced her to resign, and Sherry was actually relieved that her friend was not there to pester her with questions she had no desire to answer, but two months after Rollo's departure she had cause to call on Brenda at her flat.

'I was wondering when I'd see you,' Brenda greeted her pleasantly when she opened her door to find Sherry on her doorstep. Her pale, silky hair was tied back from her face in a simple knot, and the wide maternity dress did not hide the fact that she was in her fifth month of pregnancy. 'Is this your afternoon off?' she asked as she stood aside for Sherry to enter.

'Yes,' Sherry confirmed, studying her friend closely

when they walked into the lounge and sat down. 'You're looking well.'

'Jonathan absolutely spoils and pampers me now that I'm a stay-at-home,' laughed Brenda, then her expression sobered. 'Have you heard from Rollo?'

Sherry shook her head. 'I told you two months ago that it was over, didn't I?'

'You're looking a bit pale and washed out, and I thought maybe you had heard from him,' Brenda said, explaining the reason for her query.

An awkward silence settled between them, and Sherry clenched her hands so tightly together in her lap that her fingers went numb. She had a reason for coming to see Brenda, and what she had to say was not going to be easy.

'Brenda, I'm leaving Cape Town in two weeks' time.'

'*What?*' Brenda sat bolt upright in her chair, her face a mask of shock and total disbelief. 'I don't believe it! You've always said you'd never want to live anywhere else. What's made you change your mind now?'

'I need a change of environment,' Sherry's quiet voice continued, confusing her friend. 'I'm going to visit my aunt for a while, and I'm not sure where I'll go from there.'

'I simply can't believe it!' Brenda sat there shaking her head in continued disbelief. 'Has that business between Rollo and yourself got something to do with this decision of yours?'

Sherry forced a careless laugh past her unwilling lips. 'For goodness' sake, Brenda, why won't you believe that what I felt for Rollo was a crazy infatuation that died a swift death after his departure?'

Brenda still looked doubtful as she studied Sherry intently, then she shrugged and smiled. 'Well, I'm glad it wasn't all that serious after all.'

Sherry winced inwardly, but her features remained outwardly controlled. She disliked having to lie to Brenda, but it would be safer that way ... *much* safer!

'There's so much to do before I leave that I doubt if I'll

see you again,' Sherry said later when Brenda had made tea and they were drinking it in the lounge. 'But I'll write to you as soon as I'm settled somewhere.'

'Are you sure this is what you want to do?' Brenda asked gravely, and Sherry nodded emphatically.

'Yes, I'm sure.' Her grey eyes clouded momentarily when she put down her empty tea cup. 'There's something I would like you to do for me.'

'Name it, and it's done,' answered Brenda with a characteristic impulsiveness that almost brought a smile to Sherry's lips.

'If Rollo should ever ask, I want you never to tell him where to get in touch with me.'

Brenda's eyes widened. 'Do you think there's a possibility he might approach us for that information at some future date?'

'He may, but then again he may not,' Sherry answered. 'If he does, I would like you to withhold my address from him. Do you promise?'

'I promise.' Brenda looked solemn, but confused. 'Are you going to tell me why you don't want to see him again?'

Sherry shook her head. 'It's over, and I don't particularly want to see him again.'

'Oh, well, I suppose it's never much good raking through dead ashes, is it?' Brenda sighed.

Dead ashes! Oh, God, if only it were simply dead ashes! If only she had had more sense not to insist on that one night. If only . . . !

Sherry did not prolong her visit. She was not sure how long she could keep up the pretence, and Brenda knew her too well not to eventually suspect the true reason for her departure from Cape Town. She made her goodbye brief, and left, but it felt as if she had severed a tie with her past which she would never recapture again. It was, however, for the best. In a few months' time she would not be able to face Brenda without a sense of shame, and she did not want to be pitied.

That night, when she had bathed, she stood in front of the full-length mirror in her bedroom and loosened the bath sheet she had wrapped around her body. She let it drop to the floor while she studied her body intently. Her breasts were firm and full, but perfectly in proportion with the rest of her slender figure. Her hips were nicely rounded and her legs were shapely. She was not unhappy with the way she looked, but her grey eyes clouded when she laid her hand against her flat stomach. In a few weeks' time it would no longer be flat; it would be showing visible signs of growth, and then her shameful condition would no longer be a secret.

Sherry groaned as she turned away from the mirror to put on her nightgown. Margaret Jaeger was her only remaining relative in South Africa, and she was the only one Sherry could turn to for help and advice. Her father's sister had never married, she had made nursing her career, and after her retirement she had settled in Kromrivier, a small town in the heart of the Karoo. Aunt Margaret would know what to do, Sherry was convinced of that, and that was why she had decided to make Kromrivier her first port of call after leaving Cape Town.

The next two weeks passed swiftly, and there was an aching lump in her throat when she said goodbye to Matron Naudé and drove away from the hospital. Matron was still confused and bewildered by the sudden resignation of one of her most promising nursing Sisters, but Sherry had remained silent, giving as her only excuse the desire for a change of environment.

The arid, semi-desert Karoo lay shimmering in the heat on that March afternoon. Kromrivier was still thirty kilometres away, and Sherry was beginning to feel almost as parched as her surroundings. Fatigue was beginning to make her ache in every limb, and her eyes felt gritty behind the lenses of her dark glasses, but she did not ease her foot off the Mini's accelerator. She did not want to stop for a break, not now when she was so close to her destination, and she turned her window down to let a little more air circulate through the car. Ravens perched on telephone poles, their beaks gaping in the heat, and sheep clustered together beneath acacia trees while windmills stood motionless, waiting for a non-existent breeze.

A church spire was becoming visible beyond the distant hill, and the Mini's engine seemed to groan in protest when Sherry's foot went down a little harder on the accelerator. She was almost there and, knowing Aunt Margaret, an iced fruit drink would be awaiting Sherry on her arrival.

Time had stood still in Kromrivier, Sherry discovered some minutes later. The roads were not tarred, the shops were quaint and old-fashioned, and hens wandered aimlessly across the dusty streets to scatter with loud squawking and feathers flying when the Mini approached. Houses stood shuttered, indicating that they were used by farmers in the district as a weekend home when they came to town to do their weekly shopping on a Saturday and to attend a church service on Sunday, but the tree-lined street Sherry turned into left no doubt in her mind that the houses were inhabited by local residents.

Margaret Jaeger's house, with its small but neat garden, was like an oasis in the desert when Sherry parked in the driveway. She eased her stiff, tired body out of the car, feeling as hot and dusty as her Mini, when an elderly woman emerged from the house to welcome her with open arms.

'Sherry, it's so wonderful to see you again,' Margaret Jaeger laughed happily as they embraced, and Sherry clung for a brief moment to this slender, grey-haired woman as if she were a refuge in a storm. 'Come inside and have something cool to drink before we see to your luggage,' her aunt suggested, and they entered the whitewashed house with arms still about each other.

They had so much family and professional news to

catch up on that it was long after dinner that evening before Sherry had the opportunity to speak to her aunt about her personal dilemma and, strangely enough, it was Margaret Jaeger who gave her the opening she had been waiting for.

'When I was your age, Sherry, I would never have dreamed of spending my holiday with an old aunt who lived in a godforsaken place like Kromrivier.' The grey eyes observing Sherry were grave. 'Tell me truthfully, why did you choose to come here?'

There was no sense in beating about the bush. Her aunt was not a fool, and she would soon begin to suspect the truth. She lowered her eyes before her aunt's steady gaze, and said bluntly, 'I'm pregnant.'

If Margaret Jaeger was shocked, then a lifetime of nursing had given her the ability to show no sign of it. 'Were you raped?'

'No, I wasn't raped,' Sherry replied, her voice as calm and controlled as her aunt's. 'I was a very willing and eager partner.'

Oh, how willing and eager she had been!

'Did you love this man?'

Sherry nodded and swallowed convulsively. 'Very much.'

'But he didn't love you, is that it?' her aunt concluded.

'I thought he did, but I was wrong.' Sherry fondled her mug of coffee between her hands almost as if she was drawing strength from it. 'He left for the Antarctic two and a half months ago, and he'll be away for a year or more. If he loved me he would have wanted me to wait for him, but he was quite emphatic about our relationship ending with his departure.'

'Are you going to let him know that you're expecting his child?'

'No!' Sherry shook her head tiredly. 'That's the last thing I want to do. I don't want him to know. Not ever!'

'Far be it from me to tell you what to do,' Margaret Jaeger said after due consideration, 'but this man has the right to know that he is going to be a father. Or are you thinking of having the baby adopted?'

'Oh, no!' gasped Sherry, a measure of distaste flashing across her delicate features 'I'm going to keep my baby. It's *mine*, and it's all I . . . will have.'

'Do you think you're strong enough in mind and body to cope with the snide remarks that might come your way?'

Sherry looked up into those grey eyes observing her so intently, and her chin rose with a touch of defiance. 'I'll walk through the fires of hell, if necessary.'

Margaret Jaeger's matronly features relaxed into a smile. 'I'm very glad to hear you say that, and you will, of course, stay here with me. There's plenty of room in this house for both of us, I'll take care of you during your pregnancy, and we won't discuss the future until the baby is born.'

'Oh, Aunt Margaret!' Sherry sighed, overwhelmed by her kindness and generosity. 'I came to ask you for help and advice, but I never dreamed you would offer me so much more.'

'What's family for if we can't help each other when we are in need?' Margaret Jaeger laughed away Sherry's remark.

Sherry got up to embrace her aunt, and there was a closeness and warmth between them which had somehow never been there between Sherry and her mother. It filled her now with a pleasant warmth, and, for the first time since discovering that she was going to have Rollo's baby, she felt safe and comforted.

Margaret Jaeger was far wiser than Sherry might have imagined. She knew that work would be the antidote Sherry required most, and she knew also that one of the local doctors would shortly be requiring the services of a nurse/receptionist. She arranged an interview with Dr Gordon Shaw, and Sherry liked the man on sight. He was a tall, bulky man, a bachelor in his late thirties, and his unruly brown hair and kind hazel eyes gave Sherry the feeling that he needed to be mothered. The latter was not true, of course. He was a self-sufficient man who knew what he wanted, and Sherry's qualifications impressed him to the extent that he did not need time to consider her application.

'You start in two weeks' time,' he informed her in his gravelly voice, but Sherry felt compelled to be honest with him.

'There's one problem——' she began, but he raised a large, capable hand to silence her.

'I know you're expecting a child,' he said, leaning back in his chair behind his desk and lighting a cigarette. 'I'll arrange for a part-time help when the time comes, but this job is yours for as long as you may want it.'

'You're very kind, Dr Shaw,' Sherry smiled, and a cloud of smoke emerged almost agitatedly from his nostrils.

'I'm desperate for experienced assistance, that's all,' he said, brushing aside her remark rather fiercely, then he smiled and rose behind his desk to indicate that the interview was at an end. 'Don't forget, you start two weeks from today.'

'I shan't forget,' Sherry promised faithfully, and she left his consulting rooms to drive back to Aunt Margaret's house in a much lighter frame of mind.

Gordon Shaw became more than simply Sherry's employer during the ensuing months. He was her doctor and her friend, and he was clever and shrewd enough to delve beneath her sometimes cool exterior. The one thing she withheld from him was Rollo's name, and Gordon Shaw was tactful enough not to delve deeper than she was prepared to allow him.

Sherry's son was born on a wet October morning of that same year. The wind was a force behind that Karoo storm, but in the bedroom of her aunt's home the sun was shining especially for Sherry when the tiny, pink-faced bundle was placed in her arms for the first time. It made the hours of silent, sometimes lonely suffering worthwhile, and her future, like her arms, was no longer empty.

The months that followed were not always easy. Her aunt's home in Kromrivier had become a sanctuary, but the past was always there to haunt her, and she could not look at her baby son without seeing his father. David was the image of Rollo, and the resemblance was an agony and a pleasure which Sherry nursed secretly. She had accepted the fact that she would never see Rollo again, but the pain of it had never left her entirely. What they had had together was something she would never forget, but it was over, and she had resigned herself to the knowledge that memories were all that she had left.

It was three months after David's first birthday that Gordon Shaw took her to dinner at the local hotel one evening. This was not the first time he had invited her out to dinner, but, when Sherry sat facing him across the table in the hotel's small restaurant, she had a feeling that Gordon Shaw was going to confront her with something which she had shied away from since their first meeting. She was fond of him, but fondness and friendship were all she had to offer him, and he had never pressed for more. She could see, however, that tonight was going to be different from all their other meetings away from the surgery, and she felt tense for the first time in his company.

There were no awkward silences, but it was when they were lingering over their coffee that he steered the conversation in the direction she had feared.

'How long have we known each other?' he asked bluntly.

'Almost two years,' Sherry answered him warily, 'and you've been a good friend and employer.'

'I know what you've been through, Sherry, and I've been patient with you.'

'I'm sorry.'

His hand found hers across the table, and she looked up to find his hazel eyes resting intently on her face.

'Dare I hope that my patience will be rewarded some day?'

'I'm very fond of you, Gordon,' she said carefully, not wanting to hurt him. 'And I shall always value your friendship.'

'When a woman says that, then a man ought to know that he doesn't stand a chance, but I warn you that I don't give up that easily,' he smiled at her with a wicked look invading the warmth in his eyes. 'I shall wear you down with my patience, if nothing else.'

'Oh, Gordon,' she returned his smile sadly, 'you don't deserve to be treated this way.'

'Keep thinking that, Sherry, and it might eventually count in my favour,' he said, brushing aside her remark with a humour that hid his disappointment. 'What you really need is a holiday, and I have selfishly delayed mentioning the subject.'

'I don't need a holiday,' she protested, dreading the thought of all those days with nothing to do but think about things that did not bear thinking about.

'You're going to take a holiday all the same,' Gordon insisted. 'I've arranged for a replacement, and she'll be coming in tomorrow, so you'll have two days to show her the ropes before you go.'

'You—you mean I'm to have leave as from Monday?' Sherry stared at him aghast, and he smiled with a twinkle of humour in his eyes.

'I'm giving you three weeks,' he said. 'That's the longest I can spare you.'

Sherry was in a troubled mood when Gordon left her at her aunt's home later that evening. A holiday! What was he trying to do to her? Thrust her into a nightmare of uneventful days?

'You've had a tough time, and you deserve a break away from work,' Margaret Jaeger agreed when Sherry confronted her at the breakfast table the following morning with the news that Gordon had insisted she take a holiday.

'But what am I going to do with myself for three whole weeks?' protested Sherry indignantly.

'I'll tell you what you're *not* going to do,' her aunt informed her sternly while she poured their coffee. 'You're not taking David with you, he's too much of a handful at the moment to give you a moment's peace, and you're *not* going anywhere in that dilapidated Mini of yours.'

'I can't leave David——'

'You'll do as you're told!' Margaret Jaeger interrupted sharply, then her features and her voice softened. 'Take the train, Sherry. Go to Cape Town, visit your friends, Brenda and Jonathan, and simply relax as much as you can.'

'I don't want to go to Cape Town.'

'I know you don't want to go.' The older woman's glance rested with concern on Sherry's pale face. 'Take an old woman's advice, my dear. Go back and bury the past once and for all so that you can start thinking of the future. *Your* future and *David's* ... and perhaps also Gordon Shaw's.'

'You—you know?' Sherry asked with a start of surprise.

'My dear child, I'm not blind,' her aunt laughed shortly. 'That man has been in love with you almost since the first time he set eyes on you, but you've been too busy dwelling in the past to notice.'

'There can never be more than friendship between us,' Sherry rejected this information.

'That's what you say now, but you might feel quite differently once you've buried the past.' Margaret Jaeger reached across the table to clasp Sherry's arm affectionately. 'It's worth a try, my dear.'

Their glances met and held, and Sherry found herself thinking that her aunt might be right. It was time she buried the past, and the only place she could do that was in Cape Town.

'Very well, I'll go,' Sherry agreed at length, and a smile

of satisfaction flashed across her aunt's lined face.

'Good!' she said abruptly. 'I'm glad you're being sensible about this.'

CHAPTER FIVE

THE train sped towards Cape Town, taking Sherry further away from David and Aunt Margaret, and closer to the city she had never intended to return to. She felt tense and nervous, and not at all as if she was on her way to a relaxing holiday. Her first glimpse of Cape Town's majestic mountain was through the compartment window. It was draped in its cloth of mist, a familiar sight despite the clear blue sky, and Sherry felt the first tiny stab of excitement darting through her. Perhaps it was not going to be such a bad holiday after all.

There had been no delay *en route*, and the train arrived in Cape Town at the specified time, which was very early in the morning. An eager young man in the compartment next to Sherry's helped her with her suitcases on to the platform, but after that she insisted that she could manage on her own. She took a taxi from the station to a quiet hotel in Gardens, which was in the centre of the city, and when she had signed the register she was shown up to her room. She discovered a few minutes later that she had a clear view of the mountain from her window. She was glad about that, and she sagged down on to one of the springy beds, bouncing on it lightly like an excited child and testing it for comfort.

She still had time to go down to breakfast, but she opted instead for a bath, and exchanged her creased linen suit for comfortable slacks and a clean blouse. She brushed her hair and put on a light touch of make-up, but while she did so her glance strayed beyond her image in the mirror towards the telephone on the bedside cupboard between the beds. Should she give Brenda a call? Sherry considered this for a moment, but she finally decided against it. She needed this day alone to acclimatise herself to the knowledge that she was back in Cape Town. She would give Brenda a call the following day and arrange a meeting, but she wanted to be alone on her first day in this city with its historical background.

She took a leisurely stroll down Government Avenue, and spent some time in the museum and art gallery before she wandered through the botanical gardens where she eventually had lunch at the open-air restaurant. This had been one of her favourite pastimes when she had had a day off from the hospital with nothing better to do, but on this occasion it brought back memories of Rollo and herself feeding the pigeons and the squirrels exactly as a couple at a nearby table were doing. Sherry waited with bated breath for that familiar stab of pain, but when it came it was no more than a dull ache. Her breathing eased, and she felt herself begin to relax for the first time. It was over, the wounds were healing, and coming to Cape Town was suddenly not such a bad idea after all.

Sherry had corresponded with Brenda during the past two years, but speaking to her on the telephone was a different matter. Her letters had been written after giving each one a great deal of thought to conceal her feelings. She had simply refrained from answering some of Brenda's queries for fear that her answers might be too revealing, but confronting Brenda on the telephone, or face to face, would be something else altogether. She could not, however, leave Cape Town without seeing her friend. In doing that she would defeat the object of this holiday, but her hand still hesitated on the telephone receiver the following morning before she lifted it to her ear and asked for a line.

She dialled the number she had found in the telephone directory, and several seconds later Brenda's familiar voice answered at the other end.

'Brenda, it's Sherry,' she enlightened her friend warily.

'Sherry!' There was an excited shriek at the other end. 'Where are you calling from?'

'I'm at a hotel in Cape Town, and I was wondering if you would be at home this afternoon.'

'Of course I'll be at home!' Brenda answered at once. 'I shall expect you after lunch, and I'm looking forward to seeing you.'

'I'll see you later, then.'

Sherry replaced the receiver a moment later, and there was a hint of a smile plucking at the corners of her generous mouth. It *would* be good to see Brenda again after all this time.

She knew that Brenda and Jonathan had moved out of their flat shortly after the birth of their daughter, Mandy, and after lunch that day she took a taxi out to their home in Bloubergstrand. The view of Table Mountain from Bloubergstrand was one of the best known. It was used in travelogues, and painted often by many local and overseas artists.

Sherry asked the taxi driver to leave her at the entrance to the curved driveway leading up to Brenda's home, and arranged with him to collect her again at four-thirty. The taxi sped away, and Sherry walked up the drive towards the entrance of the house. The garden was spacious, the house architecturally modern, and it reflected perfectly the character of its owners. The front door opened, and Brenda stepped out to welcome her. Brenda was still the tall, slender young woman Sherry had known, but her pale hair was cut shorter than Sherry remembered.

'Sherry!' she exclaimed, her lovely features breaking into a delighted smile, and Sherry was caught up in a rather wild embrace. 'Oh, but it's good to see you again!'

'It's good to see you, too,' Sherry admitted when they stood back to regard each other again, then Brenda led her out of the hot sun into the cool interior of the house. 'You have a lovely home,' Sherry remarked sincerely, her glance taking in the modern furnishings.

'I'm glad you like it,' Brenda smiled, leading the way into the living-room. 'Come through here and sit down. We have so much to talk about, and there's so much I want to know that I don't quite know where to begin.'

'Where's little Mandy?' Sherry questioned her out of sheer nervousness as she lowered herself into a padded armchair and rearranged the brightly coloured scatter cushions for comfort.

'She's taking a nap at the moment, but you'll see her later,' promised Brenda, seating herself opposite her. 'Did you get the photographs of Mandy which I sent you last month?'

'Yes, thank you, they were lovely.'

They stared at each other in silence for some time, each assessing the other in a friendly, but curious manner.

'You haven't changed at all, and yet there's something about you that's different, but I can't at the moment think what it is.' Brenda was the first to voice her opinion, and Sherry felt her insides knotting with tension. 'Are you happy living with your aunt in Kromrivier?' asked Brenda.

'Very happy.' That was true in a way. She could not say that she was unhappy, but at times there was that terrible emptiness in her heart and soul which not even David could fill.

'And Dr Shaw?' Brenda questioned her inquisitively. 'What's he like?'

'He's kind and he's generous, and he's an excellent doctor,' Sherry sang his praises with honesty. 'I've enjoyed working for him.'

'Don't you ever miss the hospital routine?'

'I do sometimes,' Sherry admitted, 'but working for Gordon is never dull, and I'm always kept busy.'

'So it's *Gordon*, is it?' teased Brenda, and Sherry smiled even though her body stiffened with resentment.

'We've become friends, but nothing more.'

Brenda's glance was speculative, and Sherry could almost sense the thoughts spinning through her mind, but it nevertheless came as a shock when Brenda asked, 'I don't suppose you've heard from Rollo at all?'

This was the first time in almost two years that Rollo's name had been mentioned, and Sherry's expression matched her chilled voice. 'No, I haven't, and I never imagined I would.'

'You know,' Brenda continued, quite undeterred, 'I've never been able to shake off the feeling that you loved Rollo, and that it wasn't simply a crazy infatuation that died an instant death the moment he left Cape Town for the Antarctic.'

'You've been mistaken, Brenda,' Sherry tried to laugh off her friend's remark, but Brenda did not look as if she was convinced.

'Can you honestly sit there and tell me that, if Rollo had to walk into this room now, you wouldn't feel a thing?'

'Not a thing!' Sherry lied, and a little shiver, like a premonition, raced along her spine.

Brenda studied her speculatively, then she shrugged and changed the subject. 'How long do you intend staying in Cape Town?'

'Two weeks,' Sherry enlightened her. 'I'm planning to leave again at the end of next week.'

'We're having a party this coming Friday evening, and I'd like you to come,' said Brenda, but one look at the wary expression that flitted across Sherry's face made her laugh out loud. 'Oh, it's not one of *those* parties, Sherry. Jonathan and I have become quite staid since Mandy's birth, and Friday evening's party is no more than a get-together of friends, and we thought we'd have a *braai* if the weather lasts.' Her smile faded and her expression became pleading. 'Will you come?'

Sherry was not in the mood for a party whether it be wild or sedate, and she tried to formulate an excuse. 'I don't know if I——'

'Oh, please, Sherry!' begged Branda. 'It so happens that it's my birthday, and you've just got to come.'

The scene was familiar; achingly familiar. It reminded Sherry of that time, two years ago, when Brenda had begged her to come to her twenty-first birthday party, and she had agreed to go despite her disinclination for frivolity. That was when she had met Rollo, and her life had never been the same after that.

'I'll come,' Sherry heard herself saying just exactly as she had done two years ago, and she tried to ignore those inexplicable little shivers which were racing through her for some obscure reason.

'Oh, good!' sighed Brenda. 'Jonathan will pick you up at your hotel, and he'll take you back again later in the evening.'

'That won't be necessary,' Sherry said hastily. 'I'll get here on my own, but I would appreciate a lift back later that evening.'

'That's settled, then,' Brenda smiled, her hazel eyes alight with a strange satisfaction.

They had tea and reminisced about 'old times', and later Sherry had the opportunity to meet Mandy who was a cuddlesome, mischievous bundle of almost two. The time passed swiftly, and it felt as if Sherry had barely arrived when the taxi was there to collect her again.

'Don't forget Friday evening,' Brenda reminded Sherry when they parted in the driveway. 'And come early so that we can have a bit of time together before the other guests arrive.'

Sherry had enough time for a bath and a change of clothing when she arrived back at the hotel. She felt pleased with herself at the way she had handled that awkward topic of Rollo van Cleef, but her next meeting with Brenda still loomed ahead of her like a shadowy encounter she was not looking forward to. Those odd little shivers would race through her every time she thought about it, and it did not help to tell herself that she was being ridiculous.

The Friday evening was warm and there was scarcely a
breeze blowing when Sherry arrived at Brenda's and
Jonathan's home in Bloubergstrand. It was a perfect
night for a *braai*, and Sherry was helping Brenda in her
modernly equipped kitchen when Jonathan walked in.

'Well, well, well!' Jonathan smiled crookedly after he
had greeted her, and there was a hint of mockery in his
glance when he observed Sherry from top to toe. 'The girl
has become a woman.'

'You know, Jonathan's got something there,' Brenda
intervened, studying Sherry with renewed interest. 'You
do have a more mature look about you.'

'I am two years older since the last time you saw me,
don't forget,' Sherry tried to brush aside their
observations.

'It has nothing to do with your age,' Brenda insisted.
'You're thinner than you used to be, and yet fuller.'

'And the innocent look in your eyes has been replaced
by a look that says, "Don't touch! I've been hurt once,
and I don't intend to be hurt again",' Jonathan added his
opinion.

They were nearing the truth so rapidly that Sherry felt
alarm spiralling through her. If they delved too deeply
they might discover her well-guarded secret, and she was
not yet ready to tell them about David.

'Good heavens!' Sherry laughed forcibly. 'You're
making me feel like a specimen under a microscope in
the Path. Lab!'

Their laughter lightened the atmosphere, but that was
no guarantee that the subject would not be mentioned
again. It was at this point that Jonathan remembered his
good manners and decided it was about time he played
host.

'What will you have to drink, Sherry?'

'I think I'll have a glass of that wine you've been
warming between your hands for much too long,' she told

him drily, and a faintly embarrassed smile curved his mouth.

'Sure,' he said, opening the bottle and pouring a glass of wine for Sherry as well as Brenda.

'I saw Matron Naudé the other day,' Brenda told Sherry while she decorated the plates of snacks. 'She asked about you, and she nearly had apoplexy when I told her you were working for a doctor in private practice in some small Karoo town. She muttered, "What a waste, what a waste", and she marched off as if she couldn't bear to hear more.'

'Poor Matron Naudé,' Sherry sighed reminiscently. 'She really was quite a dear.'

'She was a dragon!' Brenda corrected, putting on a stern face to imitate the Matron. 'Nurse Lewis! When will you ever learn that a nurse's uniform should be worn with dignity and honour!'

Her mimicry was so faultless that Sherry burst out laughing, but the sound of a car coming up the drive towards the house made her sober hastily.

'I think our first guests have arrived,' Jonathan announced unnecessarily.

'Will you go out and welcome them, Jonathan?' asked Brenda, gesturing towards the salads which still needed a finishing touch. 'I have a few more things to see to here in the kitchen, so you might as well offer them a drink to get them in a party mood.'

Jonathan did as she asked without quibbling, and Sherry remained in the kitchen to lend a hand. She was not yet ready to confront the new arrivals, and she was happier for the moment helping Brenda in the kitchen. Later, when Brenda was ready to go out and meet her guests, Sherry would accompany her.

The fires were lit at dusk, and wood-smoke curled into the air. Sherry was not a stranger to some of Jonathan and Brenda's guests, and she was beginning to relax when a white Rover Sports swept up the drive. She was plagued by a vague uneasiness, but she did not pay much attention to the late arrivals, and some minutes later Brenda was ushering two people into the circle of guests standing around the fires. Sherry broke off her conversation with one of Brenda's friends, and turned, and everything inside her ground to a sickening halt when she found herself confronted by the one man she had thought she would never see again. Rollo was leaner, his face harder, and there was a coldness in those incredibly blue eyes that filled her with a sense of shock. Her face paled, and she panicked for a moment when she thought she was going to faint, but the thudding beat of her heart sent the blood rushing into her head again, and she somehow remained standing.

'Sherry, you know Rollo, of course,' Brenda announced airily while Sherry stood there as if she had been chiselled out of stone. 'And this is Delphine Ingram,' Brenda added.

Sherry forcibly dragged her attention away from the tall, dark-haired man whose ruggedly handsome features gave no indication of his feelings at that moment.

'How do you do,' Delphine Ingram greeted primly in a faintly musical voice to which Sherry added something appropriate, then the attractive blonde turned from her to face her hostess. 'Lovely place you have here, Brenda. And it's simply a divine night for a *braai*.'

'Yes, isn't it?' Brenda answered smoothly, her hazel eyes observing Sherry, but Sherry was studying the broad-shouldered man in the light grey slacks and white, open-necked shirt as if she was seeing him for the first time in her life.

'Another drink, Sherry?'

'What?' Her head snapped round, and it took a moment to focus on Jonathan who was gesturing with a bottle of wine towards the empty glass she clutched so tightly in her hand. He was looking at her oddly, and she hastily pulled herself together. 'Oh, yes, thank you, Jonathan.'

She needed something stronger than wine to settle her

nerves, but her heartbeats settled down to comparative normality when Rollo and Delphine Ingram walked away to mingle with the rest of the guests. She gulped down a mouthful of wine, aware that her hand was shaking, and she wished with all her heart that she had had the foresight to turn down Brenda's invitation. It was too late now for regrets, and she knew she had to see the evening through to the bitter end.

Sherry tried to ignore Rollo, but he was not someone who could be easily overlooked, and neither could she shut out the sound of that deep, well-modulated voice. Everything about him was too achingly familiar for comfort, but he had another woman at his side, and Sherry knew that the past would have to remain buried forever.

The fires had burned down to glowing coals, and steaks and *boerewors* were sizzling on the grids. The aroma was very mouth-watering, but Sherry had lost her appetite. The evening seemed to go on endlessly while Sherry forced herself to do the usual things such as eat and drink and laugh and talk. Her strict training as a nurse was a sturdy crutch to fall back on, and no one, not even Brenda, seemed to suspect that anything was wrong.

Sherry had shifted into the shadows surrounding the group around the swiftly dying fires when she saw Rollo walking towards her. The desire to run was incredibly strong, but she quelled it instantly. She had no reason to fear him, her secret was safe, but that did not disperse the chill of fear clutching at her heart like an icy hand.

'It's been a long time,' he said, that familiar drawl tugging her senses alive.

'Yes, it has,' she admitted coldly, incapable of reading his expression in the shadowy darkness and wondering whether his eyes still looked into hers with that icy coldness she had noticed earlier that evening.

'Two years, to be exact,' he underlined his statement as if he thought she was unaware of the time that had elapsed since their last meeting, and that angered her.

'That's correct.'

'Are you still in the nursing profession?'

'Yes,' she answered abruptly, but an uneasy sensation was beginning to spiral through her.

'But not in Cape Town.'

That was a statement, not a query, and she confirmed it with a blunt, 'No.'

'Why did you leave?'

Why all these questions? What did it matter to him whether she left, or stayed? What they had had together was in the past, and that was the way he had wanted it. Why this sudden interest in her decision to leave Cape Town?

'I needed a change of environment.' She used the same excuse she had used so many times two years ago, and it sounded just as convincing now as it had done then.

'So you went . . . where?' probed Rollo, and alarm bells started ringing in her mind, advocating caution.

'Oh, I've been all over the place,' she replied evasively, her near-frantic glance alighting on Brenda emerging from the house with an enormous tray of coffee, and she sighed inwardly with relief. 'If you'll excuse me,' she said, turning to Rollo, 'I think Brenda needs a little help.'

Rollo made no attempt to prevent Sherry from leaving, but she felt his eyes burning into her back when she walked briskly across the lawn towards Brenda.

'Why didn't you warn me that Rollo was going to be here?' she accosted her friend, making use of this brief moment alone with her.

'I didn't think it would make any difference,' Brenda said, reminding her mockingly of the rash statement she had made only a few days ago. 'Didn't you say you would feel nothing if he had to walk in unexpectedly?'

Sherry cringed inwardly at the blatant lie she had told to put Brenda off the scent, but her anger sustained her. 'I know what I said, but you could have warned me.'

'I'm sorry,' Brenda murmured sincerely, while Sherry's

glance scanned the tray in her hands.

'Shall I get the sugar and the milk?'

'Yes, please,' nodded Brenda. 'It's on the table in the kitchen.'

Grateful for something to do to ease the tension inside her, Sherry hurried inside to fetch the sugar and the milk. That did not, however, keep her occupied for more than a minute, and she was not looking forward to the rest of the evening which she knew would drag until the last of Brenda and Jonathan's guests had left.

She helped herself to a cup of coffee. It was the only thing that went down with ease that night, and she had a second cup, but it did not alleviate that inexplicable hollow at the pit of her stomach. She tried to avoid Rollo, but he came up behind her unexpectedly, and once again she had to force herself not to turn and run.

If this was a test, then she was failing it miserably. Rollo's magnetism was as potent as ever, and her senses were leaping wildly in response to his nearness.

'You were about to tell me earlier where you moved to after leaving Cape Town,' he said, picking up the threads of their conversation while he removed her empty cup from her oddly cold hands and placed it on a nearby table.

'I wasn't about to tell you anything,' she contradicted him stiffly, and his eyes appeared to be studying her intently in the darkness.

'You don't particularly want to talk to me, do you?' he mocked.

He had always had the uncanny ability to read her mind just as she had known things about him without being told. It had amused and pleased her two years ago, but now it actually frightened her.

'I don't think your lady friend particularly likes the idea either,' she countered swiftly, her grey glance darting towards the tall, lithe blonde winding her way towards them with a petulant expression on her lovely face.

'Perhaps you'll set aside an evening for me so that we can talk undisturbed,' suggested Rollo, but there was one very important reason why Sherry had no intention of letting him get close to her again.

'I think not,' she said, her voice calm and almost casual despite the tension that held her in its vicelike grip. 'We have nothing to talk about.'

Delphine reached his side at that moment, making further conversation impossible, and her speculative, coldly calculating glance raked Sherry from head to foot.

'Darling,' she purred, sliding her arm possessively through Rollo's. 'It isn't very nice of you to leave me alone among all these strange people.'

'My apologies, Delphine,' Rollo drawled, then he cast an impersonal glance in Sherry's direction. 'If you'll excuse us?'

Sherry inclined her head slightly in assent and watched them walk away from her with mixed feelings. Delphine Ingram was obviously a lady who was accustomed to having her own way, and in this respect she and Rollo suited each other perfectly.

Sherry joined the group around the dying fires, making sure she stayed far away from Rollo, but that did not prevent her glance from straying in his direction more often than she cared to remember. He was like a magnet, drawing her towards him across the crowded lawn, and no matter how much she tried she could not prevent her soul from reaching out to him. *Bury the past,* Aunt Margaret had advised, but the past, it seemed, refused to be buried. It had come rushing back at her with a stunning force, and she was not sure how she was going to cope with it. The only thing she knew for certain at that moment was that she did not want to see Rollo again, and most definitely not alone.

It was eleven-thirty when the first guests started leaving. Rollo and Delphine were among the second batch that left, and by twelve-thirty only Sherry was still there. Jonathan remained outside to make sure that the fires were out, and to clear away the chairs and tables while Sherry had a quiet cup of coffee in the kitchen with Brenda.

'You know, I can't stand that Delphine Ingram woman, and if there's any truth in the rumour that Rollo is going to marry her, then I feel sorry for him,' Brenda exploded without warning.

'Has he known her long?'

'He's been seeing quite a lot of her since his return from the Antarctic,' Brenda explained. 'Delphine Ingram's father is the head of the Scientific Research Institute, and the lady in question didn't hesitate to latch on to Rollo, who happens to be the old man's assistant. There's talk that Rollo will step into Professor Ingram's position when he retires at the end of this year, and there's also a lot of speculation about Rollo's and Delphine's relationship. As I said earlier, there might be wedding bells in the offing.'

Sherry took this news with a calmness that did not surprise her. She was beginning to feel numb inside, and there was a coldness filtering through into her veins that made her shiver inwardly.

'Are you feeling ill, Sherry?' Brenda probed anxiously. 'You're terribly pale.'

Sherry knew that the moment of truth had arrived, and somehow she found the courage to say what she should have said a long time ago.

'There's something I have to tell you,' she began, nursing her mug of coffee between her cold hands. 'When I left here almost two years ago I was pregnant.'

'I don't believe it!' exclaimed Brenda, her hazel eyes widening with shock and disbelief. 'Not you!'

Her reaction should have amused Sherry, but she felt only relief. She was, at last, opening up that festering wound, and letting the hurt flow out.

'Rollo made it clear from the start of our relationship that there had to be no commitment on either side, and I agreed. But I loved him, you see, and the night before he left for the Antarctic I...' She left her sentence unfinished, but she could see that Brenda understood, and she continued after a brief, awkward pause. 'I couldn't let him know that I was expecting his child. I didn't want him to feel under an obligation to do something about it, and I was too ashamed to tell you, so I—I decided to pack up and leave Cape Town.'

'Oh, lord, Sherry!' Brenda groaned, her face suddenly ashen. 'If only I'd known!'

Sherry was a little confused by Brenda's reaction to her news. 'There's no reason for you to be so upset about it.'

'But don't you see, Sherry?' Brenda explained in an anguished voice. 'I deliberately invited you here this evening knowing that Rollo would be coming as well. I've always been convinced that you still loved him, and I wanted to watch your reaction, but if I'd known about the baby I would never have done it.'

'You don't have to blame yourself,' Sherry hastened to reassure her. 'It's my fault entirely for not telling you the truth, but I'm relieved now that my aunt insisted I go away on holiday without David.'

'You had a boy?'

'Yes,' Sherry said quietly. 'And he's the image of his father.'

'Oh, God, Sherry, I'm sorry.' Brenda's anxious, rueful glance met Sherry's. 'What happens now?'

'I don't know,' Sherry sighed, brushing a heavy strand of golden-brown hair away from her face with a shaky hand. 'I can only hope that Rollo's relationship with Delphine is as serious as everyone seems to think, and that he leaves me alone.'

Perhaps you'll set aside an evening for me so that we may talk undisturbed, Rollo's suggestion flared in her mind, and she prayed silently that he had taken her seriously when she had declined his veiled invitation.

Sherry was in a silent, perturbed mood when Jonathan drove her back to her hotel in the centre of the city. At that time of the night there were not many cars on the road, and it seemed to take only a few minutes from the time they had left Bloubergstrand until Jonathan parked his car at the entrance to the hotel.

'Sherry . . .' His hand gripped her arm when she would have got out of the car. 'I'd like to add my apologies to Brenda's.'

'Don't feel bad, Jonathan,' she gently brushed aside his apology. 'I'm the one who was largely at fault. If I'd been honest with you and Brenda then none of this would have happened this evening.'

Jonathan's lean face looked grave. 'You know, of course, that you'll be in for a rough time if Rollo finds out that you had his child.'

'I know,' she confessed, shivering inwardly at the prospect, and hoping with all her heart that Rollo would never discover her secret.

'Take care, will you?'

'I will,' Sherry promised as she got out of his car. 'Good night, and thanks for the lift.'

CHAPTER SIX

THE warm, almost sultry, days and nights continued throughout the weekend, and Sherry made a point of being away from the hotel as much as possible. She had felt uneasy since her meeting with Rollo on the Friday evening, and she was jumpy every time the telephone rang in her hotel room. She told herself not to be silly; that the cold, impersonal look in Rollo's eyes had been sufficient evidence that he no longer cared, *if* he had ever cared, and his probing questions had merely been a form of politeness. There was no reason to believe that he would make an effort to contact her again, and yet she still felt uneasy about it.

She had walked down to the castle on the Monday

morning, she had trudged up stone steps to stand on one of the five bastions of the castle, and she had ventured down to the cells and into the notorious Black Hole where burghers of long ago had been incarcerated for plotting against the governor. The eeriness of the Black Hole remained with her when she returned to her hotel shortly before lunch, and her nerves coiled themselves into quivering knots when she received a message at the reception desk that she was to call Jonathan Hunt urgently. Her face whitened when she took the slip of paper from the girl at reception on which Jonathan's number had been written and, when she reached the privacy of her room, she immediately asked for an outside line and dialled his number.

'I thought I'd better warn you,' Jonathan said when she got through to him. 'Rollo contacted me this morning to find out what hotel you're staying at, and I couldn't withhold the information from him without making him suspicious.'

Sherry's face went a shade whiter, but her voice remained remarkably calm. 'Thank you, Jonathan.'

'Will you be OK?' he asked concernedly, awakening the first stab of real affection in Sherry.

'I'll be fine,' she reassured him. 'I'll let you know if anything happens.'

Her heart was thudding, and her hand was shaking when she put down the receiver. It was all very well to reassure Jonathan, but she was not at all convinced that she would manage to cope with the situation if Rollo should contact her. She did not want to see him again, and she could only hope that he was not going to be annoyingly persistent.

She washed and changed into a floral cotton frock and sandals before going down to lunch. The walk down to the Castle had made her hungry, but Jonathan's information had put a damper on her appetite, and she found that she could not manage more than a salad and a cup of tea.

She went up to her room after lunch, and she was still trying to decide what to do with her afternoon when the telephone rang. Her nerves leapt wildly, and her heart was beating somewhere in her throat when she lifted the receiver with a shaky hand.

'Miss Jaeger?' The girl manning the hotel switchboard sought confirmation of her identity and, when Sherry gave it to her, she added, 'There's a Professor van Cleef on the line for you. Shall I put him through?'

Sherry drew a careful, steadying breath before she said, 'Yes, thank you.'

The line clicked twice, and then Rollo's deep voice spoke into her ear. 'Hello . . . Sherry?'

'Yes,' she answered abruptly.

'I'd like you to have dinner with me this evening.' It sounded like an order rather than an invitation, and Sherry was instantly annoyed. 'There's something of importance I have to discuss with you,' Rollo added.

'I've already made other arrangements for this evening,' she lied coolly in a desperate attempt to put him off, but Rollo was very persistent.

'What about lunch tomorrow?'

'No, I——' Her mind whirled in its search for a feasible excuse. 'I'll be out all day.'

'Tomorrow evening, then?'

She was running out of acceptable excuses, and his persistence was wearing her down, but she was determined not to give in to him. 'Rollo, I really can't think of anything we have to discuss, and I don't——'

'Tomorrow evening?' he interrupted her with a challenging, authoritative note in his voice, and Sherry found herself agreeing.

'Very well, if you insist.'

'I'll call for you at seven,' he ended the conversation abruptly, and Sherry was left with a lifeless receiver in her hand which she slammed down on to its cradle in a fit of frustration and temper which she rarely displayed.

She had agreed to meet Rollo merely to get rid of him,

but she was already making plans for the following day which would put a safe and comfortable distance between them, and she hoped that this time it would be for ever.

Sherry spent the rest of the afternoon in her hotel room, making and receiving telephone calls until her plans had been confirmed. Her arrangements had been made when she gave Brenda a call that evening, and she had left nothing to chance.

'Brenda, I'm cutting my holiday short,' she explained to her friend. 'I'm leaving tomorrow afternoon.'

'Why?' Brenda demanded disappointedly.

'Rollo insists on seeing me again,' Sherry enlightened her. 'I tried to put him off, but he's persistent and, quite frankly, I'm not prepared to meet him on any terms. I can't afford to. Not now!'

'I see,' murmured Brenda understandingly.

'I can trust you to continue keeping my secret, can't I?' Sherry asked anxiously.

'You can trust us, Sherry,' came the firm reply, and Sherry felt her tense body relax to some extent.

'Thanks,' she sighed. 'I'll write to you sometime.'

They talked a while longer before saying goodbye, then Sherry hauled out her suitcase and started packing. She was going home, home to Kromrivier, David and Aunt Margaret; and ... pray God ... Rollo would not find her.

The train pulled into the Kromrivier station at six-thirty the Wednesday morning. The dew-wet earth sparkled in the early morning sunshine, and Sherry felt her heart bounce with relief and excitement when she left the dilapidated station building to take a taxi to her aunt's home. She had a ridiculous, but frightening feeling that she stood on the threshold of losing David, and she was impatient to be with him.

The front door to her aunt's home stood open, and Sherry left her suitcase in the small entrance hall. She could hear her aunt moving about in the kitchen, making breakfast, and she could hear David's gurgling baby-talk. Sherry suddenly felt intensely relieved, but she could not imagine why.

Margaret Jaeger's eyes widened with surprise when Sherry walked into the kitchen, and David's baby features were split with a smile that made his face glow. He kicked excitedly in his high-chair, and raised his plump little arms as an indication that he wanted her to pick him up. Sherry did not need a second invitation. She lifted her small son out of his chair, showered him with kisses until he giggled noisily, and hugged him tightly. His little fingers were caught in her shoulder-length hair, tugging hard in his excitement, but Sherry did not mind.

Her eyes met Margaret Jaeger's and they smiled at each other. Sherry knew her aunt well enough to know that behind that calm, enigmatic expression there lurked several pressing queries, but David was in the mood to play, and the questions would have to wait until later.

They had breakfast in the kitchen, and afterwards David played happily on the carpeted floor of Sherry's bedroom while she unpacked her suitcase. She did not want to let him out of her sight, and it was only when he showed visible signs of sleepiness that she put him in his cot, and left her room to join her aunt for tea in the shady garden at the back of the house.

'Now, I won't deny that I missed you, and so did David, but you were supposed to stay in Cape Town for two weeks,' her aunt pointed out when she had poured their tea at the slatted table beneath the shady oak.

'I couldn't risk staying longer,' Sherry explained, and she knew that there was no sense in hiding the truth from her aunt. 'I met Rollo van Cleef again when I went to a party at Brenda and Jonathan's home last Friday evening.'

A look of alarm flashed across Margaret Jaeger's lined face. 'What happened?'

'He was there with someone else, but he made the

suggestion that we meet at some time to have an uninterrupted discussion.' Sherry paused as an unexpected little shiver raced up her spine. 'I made it quite clear that I didn't like the idea, and I hoped it would end there, but it didn't. He got my address from Jonathan and telephoned me at the hotel Monday afternoon. He wanted me to have dinner with him that evening, and he said there was something he wanted to discuss with me, but I put him off by saying I had a prior engagement.'

'Which you didn't have, of course,' her aunt intervened with understanding.

'No,' Sherry confirmed, lowering her gaze to discover that she was stirring her tea with unnecessary vigour, and she carefully placed the teaspoon in her saucer before she continued speaking. 'Rollo was persistent, and I finally agreed to have dinner with him last night, but I did so simply to get rid of him.'

'So, instead of having dinner with him, you booked yourself on the first available train out of Cape Town, and when Rollo van Cleef arrived at the hotel last night the bird had flown . . . if you'll forgive the expression.'

'Yes,' Sherry answered stiffly, trying to visualise, not for the first time, how Rollo had reacted to the news that she had left the hotel.

'Do you think that was a wise thing to do?'

Sherry felt the first cold stab of uneasiness. 'I didn't stop to consider the wisdom of my decision. All I could think of was getting away.'

'I doubt if the man's a fool, and if I were in his shoes I would be extremely curious to know why you were so anxious not to see me,' Aunt Margaret voiced her opinion. 'It would make me wonder what you had to hide, and I would most certainly make it my business to find out.'

Margaret Jaeger had spoken with a wisdom and understanding of human nature which she had gathered over long years in the nursing profession, and Sherry felt the coldness of fear surging through her veins.

'Oh, God!' she groaned, her grey eyes wide and frightened in her pale face. 'I never thought of that!'

'I have never approved of the fact that he was kept in ignorance all this time, but I do believe your secret would have been safer if you'd met him instead of running away the way you did,' Margaret Jaeger said, forcing Sherry to acknowledge the foolishness of her decision to avoid seeing Rollo, and her face went a shade whiter.

'Aunt Margaret, you're frightening me!'

'That wasn't my intention, my dear,' her aunt smiled, 'and if, as you say, there's someone else in his life, then he might just shrug off your disappearance and forget about the whole thing.'

Sherry's hand was unsteady when she raised her cup to her lips and took a sip of tea. Her mind was spinning in never-ending circles, accepting and discarding facts to assuage her uneasiness, but her aunt had brought to her attention one particular fact which she could not ignore. Rollo was not a fool. He possessed a razor-sharp, keen intelligence, and her disappearance was not something he would simply shrug off and forget. She had panicked, and she had acted irrationally. She had no one else to blame but herself and, if necessary, she would have to bear the consequences of her folly.

The next few days were the worst Sherry had ever experienced. She thought of going to Gordon Shaw and asking his advice, but she decided against it in the end. This was *her* problem, and she would have to sort it out on her own, if and when the need arose.

She left the house for the first time on the Saturday morning to do some shopping. She was beginning to feel easier, less jumpy, and she had begun to convince herself that Delphine Ingram was of more importance to Rollo than someone from his past. She had, after all, made it clear to him that she had no desire to meet him privately again, and there was also no way he could find out where she lived. Brenda and Jonathan would never divulge that information, so there was no reason for her to be concerned. Why, she wondered, had she not thought of that before?

Her tension eased away, taking with it the uneasiness which had plagued her since her return to Kromrivier, and she waded through her shopping list in a much lighter frame of mind than when she had started.

She was in town much longer than she had anticipated. People stopped to talk, their friendliness and warmth something she had always been grateful for; working for Gordon Shaw had helped her to become acquainted very quickly with most of the inhabitants in this small town.

It was almost midday when Sherry turned her Mini into the tree-lined street where her aunt lived. She was looking forward to her last week at home with David and Aunt Margaret. After that it would be back to work, and then there would be only the weekends which she could spend with her son. She grimaced at the thought as she approached the house, and then an icy coldness washed over her that made her foot falter on the Mini's accelerator.

A white Rover Sports was parked in the street outside her aunt's house. It had a Cape Town registration number, and she knew the name of its owner without being told. *Rollo van Cleef.*

Sherry's hands felt like ice on the steering wheel when she parked her Mini in the short driveway at the side of her aunt's house. Her heart was thudding with fear in her breast, and her legs were actually trembling beneath her when she carried her parcels into the house.

She noticed that the lounge was empty when she left some of her packages in the hall and carried the rest into the kitchen. Through the window she could see Rollo and Aunt Margaret seated at the table under the shady oak, and David was seated on Rollo's knee, commanding their attention with his gurgling baby-talk.

Oh, God! she groaned inwardly, fighting against that unfamiliar blackness that threatened to engulf her. *Does Rollo know? Does he know that he's holding his own son in his arms?*

Her palms were damp despite the coldness which had invaded her body. She had never felt so completely disorientated before, and her movements were stiff and jerky when she stepped out of the kitchen and walked towards the three people who seemed to turn simultaneously to focus their attention on her.

Margaret Jaeger looked calm and composed except for a nervous flicker in the glance that darted from Sherry to the child which Rollo still held in his arms when he rose to his feet. Rollo's expression was shuttered, rigidly controlled, and it was this that heightened Sherry's fear. In the past she had been able to gauge his feelings, to sense the undercurrent of whatever emotion filtered through him, but now it felt as if a steel wall had been erected between them. She had known this man almost as well as she knew herself, but he had suddenly become a stranger to her.

'Hello, Sherry,' he drawled, looking down at her from his great height, and, when David leaned towards Sherry with his arms outstretched, she took him from Rollo and held him against her as if she wanted to shield him from this man who was his father.

'What are you doing here?' she demanded icily, and his sensuous mouth curved in a cynical smile.

'When you skipped out on our dinner engagement I thought I'd come and find out why.'

Sherry's glance met Margaret Jaeger's. Her aunt had been right, Rollo was not a fool, and he had done exactly what her aunt had suggested he might do.

'I'll take David inside and leave the two of you to talk,' Margaret Jaeger announced, stepping round the slatted table to take David from Sherry, and she did not wait for them to reply before she walked off into the house with the child in her arms.

'Who gave you my address?' Sherry demanded the moment they were alone, but she was afraid that she might already know the answer.

'The girl at the hotel reception desk very kindly allowed me to look it up in the register.'

Oh, damn! She had suspected Jonathan and Brenda of letting her down, and she was sufficiently ashamed of herself, but she had never once given a thought to the fact that she had written Kromrivier in the column requiring her address. That was all that was needed. Everyone in town knew her, and Rollo would have had no difficulty at all in discovering exactly where she lived.

She was angry, and she was afraid, but her face was a rigid mask behind which she hid her feelings as she repeated her query, 'What do you want?'

'Sit down and I'll tell you,' Rollo answered with a calm self-assurance she envied at that moment, but she had no intention of prolonging this meeting.

'I would prefer it if you stated your business and left,' she retorted stiffly, her body so tense that her muscles ached.

'Sit down!' The words were quietly spoken, but it was a command nevertheless, and something in his ruggedly handsome features warned her not to disobey him. She lowered herself into the chair her aunt had vacated, and perched nervously on the edge of it while Rollo pulled up his chair and seated himself close to her. There was no warmth in the blue eyes that met hers, they were cold and piercingly bright as they held her wary glance captive. 'Tell me about David,' he said in that frighteningly quiet voice.

'David?' she repeated, her voice a husky croak as panic rose like a fountain inside her.

'Yes, Sherry.' A tight smile twisted his mouth into a ruthless line that awakened a sense of foreboding. 'Tell me about my son.'

It was a warm day, but Sherry felt like a block of ice as she leapt frantically to her feet. 'You're crazy!'

'Not as crazy as you were to think I wouldn't find out,' he accused, rising to his feet to tower over her in a way that made fear clamour through her. 'I can understand now the reason for your animosity—and don't insult my intelligence by trying to tell me that he isn't my son,' he added harshly.

Trying to lie her way out of this situation would be futile. Rollo still had that uncanny ability to read her like a book, and she sagged back into her chair, resigning herself to the inevitable.

'Please go away, Rollo,' she pleaded with him as a last resort. 'Go away and leave me in peace to live my life as I see fit.'

'At this precise moment I don't particularly care how you live your life,' he answered her in that cold, harsh voice which was so unfamiliar to her. 'What concerns me now is my son's future.'

'That needn't concern you at all.'

'Oh, but it does, Sherry,' he insisted, seating himself again and pinning her to her chair with a blazing glance. 'My God, why didn't you let me know when you discovered you were pregnant?'

'You said no commitments, and I agreed. Remember?' she said, forcing herself to rake back into the past. 'When I asked you to to stay with me that night I was aware of the possibility that I might become pregnant, and when it happened, I saw no reason to involve you.'

Sherry once again had the feeling that she was being confronted by a stranger. The face was familiar, the wide-shouldered, lean-hipped body was the same, but the man inside was not the man she had known.

'What kind of cad did you take me for?' he demanded with a fury that made her face go a shade paler. 'Did you never *once* think that I might want to make arrangements for you to be taken care of until my return from the Antarctic?'

'And what would you have done then, Rollo?' she demanded, resorting to sarcasm as a form of defence. 'Would you have married me to make an honest woman of me? No, thank you! I didn't want a marriage with you, or anyone else, on that basis.'

'I couldn't care less about what you want, but that child,' he flung an arm in the direction of the house, 'is my responsibility as much as he's yours. I'm his father, he's entitled to my name, and I'm going to make sure that he gets it!'

Fear placed its icy hand over her heart. 'What are you talking about?'

'We're going to be married, whether you like it or not!' he bit out the words, and the remnants of her composure snapped into fragments.

'You must be out of your mind!' she stormed at him, leaping to her feet once again only to find that Rollo had risen also to dominate her with his sheer height and breadth.

'I don't want that child to go through life thinking he had a father somewhere who never cared whether he lived or died,' Rollo informed her with a controlled fury that made her shudder inwardly at the thought of what he might do if he unleashed it completely. 'David is *mine*!' he added almost savagely. 'I took your virginity, and in the process I helped to make him. *And* he's going to know it. Do I make myself clear?'

'What about Delphine Ingram?' Sherry sought escape from this situation which was fast becoming a nightmare. 'I thought you had plans to marry her?'

Rollo's mouth tightened ominously. 'That will just have to wait now, won't it.'

'Do you think she'll be happy with this cancellation of your plans?' Sherry pressed on desperately.

'My personal needs are irrelevant at the moment,' came the biting reply, 'and Delphine will have to understand and accept that.'

I wonder, thought Sherry somewhat cynically. Delphine Ingram was not a woman who would take kindly to someone thwarting her plans, and most especially not where Rollo was concerned.

'I'm not going to marry you!' she shouted, resorting to fury when all else failed to convince Rollo. 'I'm not going to marry you, and you can't make me because there's no legal argument you could use to lay claim on David.'

'I wouldn't be so hasty in declining my proposal of marriage, if I were you,' he warned calmly. 'When David is old enough to ask questions he'll want to know why you deprived him of the opportunity to get to know his father, and when he seeks me out I'll not withhold the truth from him. I'll tell him that it's his mother's fault he had to be ridiculed by other children during his young life, and you'll lose him, Sherry. Think it over,' he suggested, 'and I'll be back this evening to hear what you've decided.'

He turned on his heel and strode away, leaving her almost gaping incredulously as she stared after him. Her mind issued frantic instructions, insisting that she follow him into the house and have it out with him now, but her limbs felt as if they had been filled with lead and they refused to obey.

Sherry had no idea how long she stood out there in the dappled sunlight with her face as white as her cotton blouse, and her heart pounding out a rhythm of fear against her ribs. Two years ago she would have leapt at the chance to marry Rollo, but not now, and not because he felt under an obligation to do so. The mere thought of it was abhorrent to her, but his warning had struck deep. David was *hers*. He was *her* responsibility, and Rollo had no right at all to step in and interfere. But what if Rollo's prediction came true?

Rollo had left by the time Sherry entered the house, and she was never sure afterwards how she got through the next hour until David was asleep in his cot.

'How did Rollo find out that David was his child?' she asked without raising her glance from the sleeping child when her aunt walked into her room.

'Do you really need me to answer that?' Margaret Jaeger counter-questioned, joining Sherry beside the cot and looking down at David who had curled his fingers up beneath one rosy cheek.

Sherry studied her child anew, but she knew the answer without being told. The dark hair, the long lashes hiding those very blue eyes, and those childish features with the suggestion of a dimple in the chin spoke for themselves. David was Rollo's child, and Rollo would have had to be blind not to realise it.

'I've made a pot of tea,' her aunt interrupted her thoughts. 'Let's go into the kitchen, then we can talk without waking David.'

Sherry nodded without speaking and followed Aunt Margaret out of the room and down the short passage into the kitchen. They seated themselves at the table, and her aunt poured the tea into the delicate China teacups she loved so much. Sherry drank hers black on this occasion, and added an extra spoon of sugar. She needed something to settle her nerves. Or was it perhaps shock that had left that shaky feeling at the pit of her stomach?

'I gather he wants to marry you,' Margaret Jaeger broke the silence between them, and Sherry forced down a mouthful of hot tea before she answered.

'Yes, he does.'

'And you don't want to marry him.'

'No, I don't,' Sherry stated firmly, 'and he can't make me.'

'You're thinking about yourself, and you're not taking David into consideration,' her aunt accused.

'On whose side are you, Aunt Margaret?'

'I'm on your side and David's,' her aunt assured her. 'You want only the best for David, don't you?'

'Yes, but——'

'A boy needs his father, Sherry,' her aunt pointed out wisely. 'There's also the question of his education. You earn a good salary, but you could never give him the opportunities his father could give him. Are you going to deprive your son of these opportunities by refusing Rollo's proposal?'

Sherry squirmed inwardly. 'That's not a fair question.'

'It may not seem fair to you at the moment, but I suggest you consider it seriously before Rollo returns this evening.'

Sherry did consider it. She spent the rest of that afternoon tearing herself apart inside with the knowledge that both Rollo and her aunt had put up a strong argument. She wanted the best for David. She also did not want to lose him. If she married Rollo, then he would make sure that his son had the best, and there would be no cause for her to be accused of deprivation, but what a price she had to pay to achieve this. Oh, God, what a price!

Rollo arrived at seven that evening. Margaret Jaeger let him in, and then discreetly disappeared to leave Sherry alone with him in the small lounge with its old-fashioned furniture and well-worn carpet. Sherry was standing beside an old copper urn which her aunt had salvaged at one of the hospitals where she had worked, and her face was pale though composed when she faced Rollo across the room. He was dressed almost exactly the same as when she had seen him the very first time. The blazer was blue, but his slacks were a lighter shade of blue instead of grey, and she felt again that tightness at the pit of her stomach.

'Well?' Rollo demanded, and he was not referring to her feelings at that moment. He wanted an answer, and he knew very well there was only one answer she could give him.

'I'll marry you,' she said stiffly, 'but I want to make it very clear that I'm marrying you solely for David's sake.'

'I never imagined you would agree for any other reason,' he mocked her. 'The only matter left to discuss is how soon will you marry me?'

'I can't answer that until I've spoken to Dr Shaw,' she said, lowering her gaze to the strong column of his throat where his white shirt had been left unbuttoned. 'It would depend on how soon he could arrange for a replacement.'

She did not relish the thought of confronting Gordon

with the news that she was going to leave him to marry Rollo, but she would think about that later.

'Then I trust you will let me know as soon as you discover when you'll be free so that I may make the necessary arrangements?' Rollo asked, interrupting her perturbed thoughts. 'I'm staying at your local hotel, and the length of my stay will depend entirely on you.' He eyed her somewhat threateningly. 'And don't try to escape me again!'

She had witnessed his fury that morning before lunch, and she had no desire to witness it again. She nodded, incapable of speech at that moment, and Rollo left the house moments later.

CHAPTER SEVEN

SHERRY had the opportunity to see Dr Gordon Shaw at his consulting-rooms on the Monday morning at a time when there was a break in the flow of patients. She had not been looking forward to this confrontation, but it could not be delayed.

'I heard through the grapevine that you were back earlier than expected,' Gordon smiled at her warmly when they sat facing each other across the wide expanse of his desk. 'I would have called in to see you, but I've been rushed off my feet with this stomach virus which seems to be plaguing everyone.'

'You don't have to apologise,' Sherry reassured him, knowing only too well how hectic a doctor's life could be at times.

'I've also heard that you have a visitor from Cape Town staying at the local hotel,' he added, startling her with his knowledge.

He had inadvertently given her the opening she had sought, and she saw no reason to delay the reason for her visit, but she was suddenly as nervous as a student nurse on her first day on ward duty.

'There's something you have to know,' she began, lowering her eyes as she scraped her flagging courage together. 'It's very important to me that I should be the one to tell you this, and that you don't eventually hear it from someone else.'

'Whatever it is, Sherry, you know you can always rely on my support.'

She felt tears stinging her eyelids, and she blinked them away hastily. Gordon was being kind, as always, and she was going to repay his kindness with something she knew would hurt him. Oh, how she hated herself at that moment!

There was no sense in the use of delaying tactics. It might work with some, but not with Gordon Shaw, and Sherry came directly to the point. 'My visitor happens to be David's father, Professor Rollo van Cleef.'

She could not look at Gordon, but she heard the sharp intake of his breath while she sat there staring unhappily at the side panels in the solid mahogany desk.

'I think I've heard of him,' he said, recovering swiftly. 'Wasn't he the leader of a group of scientists and marine biologists who went to the Antarctic two years ago?'

'Yes.' Sherry looked up at his shuttered eyes. 'He wants me to marry him as soon as possible.'

Gordon nodded abruptly. 'I can understand his haste, and I applaud it, but your presence will be missed here in my consulting-rooms.'

Sherry did not say anything. What *could* she say?

'Does David look like his father?'

His query was unexpected, almost as if he was determined to hurt himself, and she nodded slightly.

'How do you feel about this man? Do you still love him?' She raised her startled glance and saw a look of rare impatience flash across Gordon's face. 'I think I have the right to know, Sherry.'

'I—I don't know how I feel,' she stammered helplessly.

'I always believed that—that I still loved him, but now that I've seen him again I find him so changed that he's almost like a stranger to me. It—it's quite frightening.'

Gordon got up behind his desk and came at once to her side to take her hands in his. 'You don't have to be afraid. I know you once loved him very much, and you might find you still feel the same about him now, but I want you to remember that I shall always be here if you should need me.'

'Do you have to be so kind to me when I've done nothing but hurt you?' she demanded, a wave of irritation sweeping through her when she looked up at him, and his smile deepened.

'I'm being kind for a very good reason,' he told her in his calm, gravelly voice. 'If Rollo van Cleef doesn't make you happy, then I shall soon know about it, and I'll put up a fight for you, Sherry, because I consider you're worth fighting for, so don't say I didn't warn you.'

Sherry could not decide what her feelings were at that moment. Any other woman would have been delighted at the knowledge that a man like Gordon Shaw wanted her so badly he was prepared to fight for her, but Sherry could only conjure up a feeling of dismay.

'How soon do you think you could release me from my duties?' she forced the conversation back on to a business level.

'Immediately,' came the abrupt reply, and Sherry did not linger to ask how he would manage. It had been awkward enough having to tell him about her marriage plans, and the only thing that remained was for her to let Rollo know that she was free to marry him whenever he wished.

The latter was something she dreaded, and the only consoling thought she had to cling to was that she was doing this for David's sake.

Sherry preferred to confront Rollo on neutral ground rather than in her aunt's home, and she drove directly to the hotel. He was sitting on the veranda, his long, muscular limbs encased in blue denims, and the sleeves of his white shirt rolled up to his elbows. An empty whisky glass stood on the small table beside him, and the menace in his narrowed eyes made her falter momentarily as she walked up the steps towards him.

'This is an unexpected pleasure,' he smiled twistedly, rising to his feet, and Sherry wondered whether coming to see him at the hotel had been such a good idea when she felt her heartbeats quicken alarmingly.

'Is there somewhere we could talk privately?'

Rollo cast a wry, critical glance along the crowded veranda. 'The only privacy we'll have in this godforsaken place is in my room.'

Hard fingers gripped her arm before she could object, and she was marched quickly into the hotel, and up the creaky stairs to a small room overlooking the dusty street where the general dealer was sandwiched in between the bakery and the mill.

'Panoramic view, isn't it?' Rollo remarked derisively. 'But you didn't come here to admire the view, did you?'

Sherry had wanted to meet him on neutral ground, but she had not imagined she would be thrust into such intimate surroundings as his hotel bedroom, and her throat tightened with nervousness. Rollo was so vitally male, and she resented the way her senses seemed to respond to that magnetism he exuded.

'Well?' he prompted laconically, hooking his thumbs into the belt hugging his denims to his lean hips, and Sherry pulled herself together with an effort.

'I'm free to marry you whenever you wish.' The words came out in a rush before she gave herself time to change her mind.

'I haven't much time to waste,' he told her curtly. 'I'll make the necessary arrangements for this coming Saturday, and we'll have to leave for Cape Town immediately afterwards.'

Sherry felt her throat tighten once again. 'Does it have to be so soon?'

'The sooner the better.' His mouth twisted in a tight, angry smile as if he had probed her thoughts. 'You won't find it all that difficult being married to me.'

Fingers of steel bit into her shoulders, jerking her up against his hard body and, caught unawares, she was totally defenceless when his hard, sensuous mouth settled on hers with a force that drove her lips apart for the intimate invasion of his tongue. Little shivers of unwanted pleasure cascaded through her, awakening emotions which had lain dormant for so long, and her body went limp against his even while her mind rejected it.

She stood swaying when he released her, her breathing fast, and, humiliatingly, she had to clutch at him for support, the bulging muscles in his arms rippling beneath her fingers.

'See what I mean?' Rollo taunted her mockingly, and a swift tide of anger gave her the necessary strength to step away from him.

'I hate you, Rollo!' she seethed, her cheeks flushed with fury and embarrassment. 'I hate you for what you're doing to me!'

'Rest assured, Sherry,' he returned harshly, 'the feeling is mutual.'

Sherry and Rollo were married on the Saturday in the small stone chapel nestling amongst the cypress trees. It was one of those hot days in the Karoo when hardly a breeze blew, and Sherry could feel the perspiration breaking out all over her body beneath her beige linen suit where she stood in front of the pulpit with Rollo. She was clutching the posy of pink carnations which Aunt Margaret had insisted upon, and her heart was drumming so loudly against her temples that she could barely hear the minister's voice prompting her in her responses.

Rollo stood beside her, tall and austere in a dark, expensively tailored suit. His face was expressionless, his eyes hooded, and his deep voice was clipped whenever he was required to speak. He was the man she had loved so desperately two years ago; he was, she had believed, her soulmate, but now there was no communication of the mind and the spirit. There had been no need once to reach out to make contact, it had been there between them, an instant recognition, but she was beginning to think her beautiful memories had been nothing but a dream.

A plain gold band, cold and hard, was slipped on to the ring finger of her left hand. Rollo's touch had been impersonal, but an electrifying sensation had surged through her, sweeping her back into the past until she was standing on the balcony of Brenda's flat with Rollo's touch trapping her, and drawing her into that world of alien sensations from which she had wanted never to escape.

Rollo turned to face her when the ceremony had ended, but Sherry could not look at him. She was afraid of what he might see in her eyes while she fought to control herself. She had had more than enough proof, that day in his hotel room, that she could still respond to him physically, but she was not going to give him the satisfaction of seeing just how deeply she was affected by him. She had entered into this marriage for the sake of their child, there was no guarantee that there would not be a second parting, and she had to remember that.

Sherry accepted Aunt Margaret's congratulations with a cynicism which had manifested itself in her during the past two years. She was, after all, marrying Rollo only for the sake of the child which had resulted from that one foolish night they had spent together, and not for the usual reasons marriages were perpetrated.

The minister's wife added her signature to the register as a second witness to their marriage, and then they were walking out of the chapel into the stinging, midday heat. There was a piercing quality to the shrill sound of the cicadas, and deep inside Sherry something screamed out in response.

'We shall have to leave as soon as possible,' Rollo announced when they were returning to Aunt Margaret's house. 'It's a long drive back to Cape Town, and I'd like to get there this evening.'

Sherry cast an anxious glance over her shoulder at her aunt seated in the back of the Rover Sports, and Margaret Jaeger smiled back reassuringly.

'I shall miss you,' her aunt said some time later when she was saying goodbye to Sherry and David, and tears mingled with her smile.

'We shall miss you, too,' Sherry assured her, having difficulty in hiding her own tears when she hugged her aunt. 'I shall never be able to thank you enough for everything you did for me, and for David,' she whispered as she emerged from their embrace.

'Neither shall I be able to thank you enough for taking care of Sherry when she needed you,' added Rollo.

Sherry glanced up at the man beside her who was now her husband, and she found it rather odd that he should have said something like that. Had he really meant it, or had he merely said it to impress her aunt? There was a time when it would not have been necessary for her to wonder. She would have known. But now there was that unseen barrier between them, and it was impenetrable.

She had not said goodbye to Gordon Shaw, Sherry remembered as they drove away from Kromrivier, but perhaps it was better this way. As much as Gordon might want to help her, there was nothing he could do to alter the fact that she was now Rollo van Cleef's wife, and the only one who could determine her future was Sherry herself.

It was her immediate future that troubled her most at that moment. How would his friends and colleagues receive her? And, more to the point, how was Delphine Ingram going to react to the presence of another woman in Rollo's life?

Her arms were beginning to ache with David's weight. He was asleep, his dark head nestling against her breast,

and Sherry kissed him lightly on the forehead before she
asked Rollo to stop the car so that she could put David on
the back seat.

'Stay where you are,' Rollo instructed when he had
pulled off the road, and got out to walk round to her side.

David did not stir when Rollo lifted him out of Sherry's
arms and made him comfortable on the back seat of the
Rover, and a few moments later they were once again
speeding towards Cape Town.

Rollo made no attempt to ease the tedium of the long
journey with polite conversation. There had, Sherry
realised, been very little communication between them
since the Monday when she had stormed out of his hotel
bedroom. He had made the necessary arrangements on
his own, consulting her only briefly on the legal details,
and she had spent less than half an hour with him in the
local jeweller's shop to select a wedding ring.

It was, therefore, a long and virtually silent trip to
Cape Town with only a few stops in between. The
scenery was beautiful, once they had left the Karoo
behind them, and it was particularly beautiful at sunset
when they drove through high mountain passes and
down into valleys of vineyards, but Sherry was intensely
relieved when she glimpsed Cape Town's lights flicker-
ing in the distance. She was tired and tense, and David
had become so restless that she had to take him on to her
lap in an attempt to keep him quiet.

Rollo drove out to Constantia, and the name 'Five
Oaks' was carved into the concrete pillars at the entrance
to the long drive up to the gabled house she still
remembered. She could not see much in the darkness, but
there would be plenty of time for an intensive exploration
of her new environment, and she had to admit that she
was more than curious to see more of Rollo's home.

The heavy oak door with its brass knocker was opened
before they reached it, and a coloured woman in a blue
overall and white apron admitted them. She was not a
stranger to Sherry, this buxom woman with the greying

hair, and her dark gaze darted from Rollo to rest with recognition on Sherry.

'Good evening, Connie,' Rollo addressed the coloured woman whom Sherry had met briefly two years ago, then he gestured towards Sherry, who was trying to control the very tired and irritable little boy in her arms. 'I'd like you to meet my wife, and my son, David, who isn't in the best of moods at the moment.'

The pride in his voice when he spoke about David was unmistakable, and Sherry felt a little of the ice melt around her heart.

'I'm pleased to meet you again, madam,' the coloured woman smiled politely at Sherry, and there was an almost motherly warmth in her eyes when they settled for a moment on the child in Sherry's arms.

'Were the rooms prepared as I instructed?' Rollo questioned Connie while Sherry cast a quick glance about the spacious, carpeted hall with the old-fashioned chandeliers hanging from the high ceiling. Everything was still as she remembered it.

'Yes, Professor,' the woman assured him. 'If you'd like to go upstairs, I'll get George to bring in your suitcases.'

Rollo nodded abruptly, and gestured Sherry towards the stairs leading to the upper floor. Her hand gripped the intricately carved wooden balustrade for support as she walked up the carpeted stairs with Rollo. On the landing between the two floors she glimpsed a tall Japanese Imari vase on a table against the wall. The flowery pattern on the vase was exquisitely painted in blue, red, black and gold, and Sherry, despite her limited knowledge, knew that it had to be old and priceless. She would have to keep an eye on David at all times, she told herself. She would never forgive herself if he should break anything so beautiful; a vase like that would be irreplaceable.

Sherry was directed towards the left when they reached the upper floor, and Rollo pushed open the first door on their right as they walked down the passage.

'This will be David's room,' he informed her in that abrupt voice which was so unfamiliar to her.

She found the light switch against the wall and stared in silence at the room which had been decorated with all the modern equipment for a nursery. Rollo had obviously gone to a great deal of trouble to have this room prepared for their arrival, and she could not let this discovery pass without making him aware of her appreciation. 'This is a lovely room, and I'm sure David is going to be very happy here.'

His eyes flickered strangely. 'And you, Sherry? Will you be happy here at Five Oaks?'

'My happiness is of no consequence,' she answered stiffly, putting David down on the carpeted floor and letting him crawl around to investigate on his own. 'I'm here because of David, and if he's happy, then that's all that matters.'

'How self-sacrificing of you,' Rollo mocked her derisively, making her anger rise sharply, but David demanded her attention at that moment, and everything else was set aside as she picked him up in her arms and tried to pacify him.

Connie walked into the nursery at that moment and held out her arms to the tearful little boy. His crying stopped at once as he looked into her smiling face, and Sherry was amazed when he allowed himself to be taken from her arms.

'I love children, madam,' Connie explained as if she sensed Sherry's amazement. 'I have six children of my own, and I'm a grandmother of four.'

'Then David is obviously in good hands,' Sherry smiled at her with some relief.

Connie grinned broadly and nodded. 'Your suitcases are in the master bedroom, madam. If you'll show me which one is *kleinbaas* David's, then I'll see that he is fed and put to bed while you and the Professor prepare yourselves for dinner at eight-thirty.'

The master bedroom. Sherry felt a terrible anxiety

clutching at her insides, but Rollo was already taking her
arm and leading her down the passage and into that room
which was so achingly familiar to her.

She wanted to speak, but no sound passed her lips as
voices, like ghosts from the past, echoed through her
mind. *You're making me wonder why I got myself involved
in this crazy set-up in the first place, and why I should bother
to see you again,* she heard her own anguished voice
crying out, and it was followed swiftly by Rollo's stinging
reply, *I'm beginning to wonder that myself!*

She tried to pull herself together, pointing out David's
suitcase to a waiting Connie, and she glanced about her
nervously once she was alone again with Rollo.

'I have a few telephone calls to make,' Rollo's
announcement intruded on those ghostly voices from the
past. 'I'll meet you again downstairs for dinner.'

He turned on his heel, striding out of the room before
she could say anything, and she stared about her in
thoughtful silence, her mind in a turmoil.

The room had been redecorated since the last time she
had seen it. A magnificent four-poster bed dominated the
room, and a lemon satin quilt had replaced the blue silk
bedspread. The heavy curtains at the windows were a
floral mixture of green and gold, and the carpet, with its
thick pile, was a soothing olive-green. The enormous
teak wardrobe had a full-length mirror down the one
panel, and it matched the dressing-table. Both pieces
definitely dated back a hundred years or so, but her
glance was irrevocably drawn once again towards the
four-poster bed in the centre of the room. One could get
lost in a bed that size, she thought, a nervous giggle
bursting past her lips. Unless . . . !

She shut her mind to the obvious and concentrated on
her surroundings. Rollo was obviously fond of collecting
old furniture and ornaments. That was something she
had not known about him, but she supposed she would
discover many more things about this man she had
married.

Married. It sounded odd to think of herself as being married. She did not feel married. The arrangements and the wedding itself had been carried out in such an impersonal way that, if it were not for the unfamiliar weight of that ring on her finger, she could almost have made herself believe she had dreamt it all.

It had been a traumatic day, one way and another, but there was no time to pause for thought. Within less than an hour she would have to be downstairs for dinner, and she needed a bath and a change of clothing.

She emerged from the white-tiled bathroom twenty minutes later, but the brief soak in a hot bath had done nothing to ease her tension at the thought of dining alone with Rollo. Think of this as an adventure, she told herself in an attempt to boost her confidence and her morale, but somehow there was nothing adventurous about living in the same house with a man whom she had married simply because he was the father of her child.

Sherry slipped into a floral silk dress which was cool and comfortable, and left her hair pinned up until she had applied a little make-up to her pale face. She could not go downstairs looking like a ghost, she told herself as she added an extra touch of blusher to her prominent cheekbones.

'Oh, God!' she groaned, pulling the combs from her hair to let it fall in a silken mass to her shoulders. 'What have I got myself into now?'

She brushed her hair vigorously and added a touch of her favourite perfume behind her ears. She was ready outwardly, but her insides were suddenly quivering with nerves as she left the master bedroom and walked down the passage towards the nursery.

David had been bathed, and he was sitting in a high chair, spoon-feeding himself quite contentedly while Connie lent a helping hand.

'Mama!' he said excitedly when he saw Sherry, and she stepped up to him quickly to drop a kiss on his dark curls.

'Be a good boy for Mummy.'

'Good boy,' he echoed proudly.

'You go down and have your dinner, madam,' Connie suggested. 'I'll stay with *kleinbaas* David until he is asleep.'

Sherry nodded and left the nursery. She was not in a hurry to go downstairs, but when she glanced at her watch she realised that she could not delay it much longer.

She found her way down to the living-room with comparative ease, but her heart leapt uncomfortably in her breast when she entered the spacious room to see Rollo taking a bottle of champagne out of the refrigerator section of a tall oak cabinet.

He turned at that moment, and his blue gaze met hers across the length of the room. His white shirt was open at the throat, and his brown slacks were moulded to his lean hips and muscular thighs as he put down the bottle and walked towards her. He had showered and changed, possibly in one of the guest-rooms, and her heart thudded heavily, almost choking off her breath as her diabolical mind conjured up memories she would have given anything not to recall at that moment; memories of that magnificent body against her own, and the smoothness of his skin stretching across rippling muscles.

'You're not about to faint, are you?' demanded Rollo, a hint of mockery mingling with the concern in his deep voice.

Sherry gripped the back of a padded armchair with a trembling hand and leaned against it slightly in an attempt to regain her much needed composure. This was not the time to go to pieces, she warned herself, and her years of rigid training in the wards came to her rescue. Her heartbeat slowed down, and her breathing became more regular, but a thin film of perspiration stood out on her forehead with the effort she had put into it. She had to think of her marriage to Rollo as simply another job, and she was not going to let her personal feelings become involved in it.

'I must be tired,' she murmured, trying to explain away her behaviour.

'And afraid.'

'Afraid?' she echoed, her startled glance rising to meet his, and her pulse rate quickening with something close to fear.

'My dear, this is our wedding night,' he reminded her mockingly. 'Don't tell me you've forgotten?'

'It's not something I'm likely to forget,' she answered coldly, getting a firmer grip on herself.

'You needn't be afraid, though,' Rollo assured her with that biting mockery that stung like the lash of a whip. 'I married you to get my son, and that's all that interests me at this moment.'

His son! She knew he had married her solely because she had had his child, and she had agreed. But why did it have to hurt so much?

'I imagine that *is* all that interests you at the moment,' she answered him with a calmness she had dredged from somewhere, and he studied her raised face with a burning intensity in his blue eyes before he turned from her to open the bottle of champagne he had taken out of the oak cabinet's refrigerator.

Sherry took this moment to glance about her. The cream-coloured curtains drawn across the tall windows were of a heavy woven fabric. The thick pile of the carpet was of the same colour, and the padded chairs and sofa were a pale, dusky blue in contrast. A child could create havoc in such elaborately furnished surroundings, she thought for the second time since her arrival at Five Oaks. She would have to keep a constant eye on David if she did not want any unfortunate mishaps occurring.

The champagne cork shot out of the neck of the bottle, making her flinch visibly. Her legs were beginning to feel like jelly, and she lowered herself into a chair beside a round, marble-topped table when Rollo turned and walked towards her with a glass of champagne in each hand.

That constant accusation in his eyes whenever he looked at her was beginning to bite deeper and deeper into her soul until an overriding guilt took possession of her. He handed her a glass of champagne and lowered his long, muscular length into the chair facing hers.

'Shall we drink a toast to our future as a family unit?' he suggested, raising his glass, but Sherry shook her head.

'Perhaps it would be more appropriate to drink a toast to the sacrifices we both had to make to form this family unit.'

A cynical smile twisted his mouth. 'What did you have to sacrifice, Sherry?'

'Just as you had to sacrifice your marriage to Delphine Ingram, I had to sacrifice the possibility of finding happiness with a man I respected and admired very much.' There was a grain of truth in that, she tried to console herself.

'Respect and admiration!' snarled Rollo with a savage mockery. 'Was that all you felt for Gordon Shaw?'

'What I felt for him is none of your business!' she struck back at him.

'Perhaps so, but let me tell you this, my dear Sherry,' he countered swiftly with a ruthless twist to his mouth that frightened her. 'Admiration and respect mean absolutely nothing in a marriage unless there is also a fire lit between the man and the woman. We had that fire once, and we might find it again, but until then . . .' He paused significantly and raised his glass. 'Shall we drink to the future?'

Sherry remained silent, her cheeks burning as if the fire he had mentioned had been lit in her face, and she raised her glass to her lips to take a sip of the sparkling liquid, hoping it would steady those butterflies at the pit of her stomach.

'Dinner is ready to be served, Professor,' a young

coloured woman spoke from the doorway, and Rollo rose at once to his feet.

'Thank you, Bettina,' he smiled briefly, picking up the bottle of champagne he had placed on the table beside his chair and gesturing towards the door. 'This way, Sherry, and bring your glass with you.'

The dining-room was across the hall from the living-room, and Sherry could not help but admire the long stinkwood table with the matching antique dresser. There was a certain unreality about being in Rollo's house, and she knew it would take a little time to adjust to the knowledge that this was now *her* home as well.

Rollo was seated at the head of the table with Sherry on his left. The silverware glittered on the lace tablecloth, and the scent of the roses in the shallow vase was almost sickeningly sweet while they sipped their champagne and waited for their first course to be served. Sherry had never known such luxury in a home, and it completely overawed her.

'You're not eating, Sherry,' he accused when they were halfway through their meal. 'Has the dinner not been prepared to your satisfaction?'

She stared at the succulent lamb and garden-fresh vegetables on her plate, and said apologetically, 'Everything has been superbly prepared, but I'm not very hungry.'

'The servants are aware of my preferences,' he continued with that hint of mockery in his voice that made her hackles rise, 'but, as my wife, you will naturally have the authority to make whatever changes you wish where the menus and the household duties are concerned.'

'Thank you,' she responded stiffly, losing her frail appetite completely, 'but I have no intention of rushing in and altering a routine which is obviously running smoothly, *and* to your satisfaction.'

His mouth tightened. 'This is now your home, Sherry, and I trust you will make it as comfortable for yourself as it is for me.'

Home, to Sherry, was still Margaret Jaeger's small house in Kromrivier, and it would take quite some time before Five Oaks felt that way to her.

She changed the subject, putting down her knife and fork and making no further attempt to eat. 'I haven't seen much of your home, Rollo, but what I have seen so far has really impressed me.'

Rollo shrugged slightly, indicating to Bettina that their plates could be removed. 'Some of the furniture I have here might be a trifle old-fashioned——'

'Antique and beautifully preserved,' Sherry interrupted him, 'but never old-fashioned.'

Bettina had cleared the table quietly and they were alone in the dining-room as a look of surprise flashed across Rollo's ruggedly handsome face. 'You like antiques?'

'In the right setting,' she admitted, 'and you have a perfect setting for it here at Five Oaks.'

'It appears there's much I still have to discover about the wife I've acquired in such a hurry,' he remarked with that hateful, ever-present mockery curving his sensuous mouth as he reached for the champagne bottle. 'More champagne?'

'No, thank you.'

'But I insist.' He replenished her glass as well as his own, then put the bottle on the ice and raised his glass in salute. 'I'd like to drink a toast to you, Sherry.'

'To me?' she asked warily.

'You're a very beautiful woman,' he explained smoothly, 'and collecting beautiful things has always held a certain fascination for me.'

Sherry felt the blood drain slowly from her cheeks. 'Am I being classified among your *objets d'art*?'

'Do you mind?' he smiled, his blue gaze trailing across her bare shoulders, and lingering insolently where her breasts strained against the silk bodice of her dress.

'I'm not an ornament, nor an antique,' she protested,

her body taut with resentment.

'Would you rather be used than admired?'

She felt the blood flood back into her cheeks with a pulsating force. To be used by Rollo, in the sense he meant, would be the final insult. Her anger rose sharply, but she forced herself to put a damper on it.

'If you're trying to trap me into saying something I might regret, then I'm not taking the bait,' she answered him with a calmness that belied the raging fury inside her.

'Clever girl,' he laughed softly, pushing back his chair and rising to his feet. 'Shall we return to the living-room?'

Sherry left her glass of champagne untouched on the dining-room table as she accompanied Rollo across the hall into the living-room where a tray of coffee had been placed on a low table between the chairs where they had sat before dinner.

'Will you pour?' Rollo asked when they were seated, and Sherry nodded, perching rigidly on the edge of her chair while she poured their coffee from the silver coffee pot.

'Black with no sugar,' she said as she passed Rollo his cup. 'Am I correct?'

'You have a good memory,' he smiled faintly, his lazy eyes hooded as his glance flicked over her, 'but then so have I.'

She felt him stripping her, divesting her mentally of every scrap of clothing, and once again she had to suppress that surge of anger that rose inside her.

'How long were you in the Antarctic?' she tried to steer the conversation in a safer direction.

'We stayed for fifteen months.' He studied her intently over the rim of his cup while he swallowed down a mouthful of coffee. 'Did you ever think of me?'

'Not very often,' she lied, not daring to raise her glance while she sipped at her own coffee.

'I thought of you,' he surprised her with his statement.

'During idle moments in below zero temperatures a man tends to think of warm arms and tender lips, and, God knows, those conditions allowed for plenty of time to think and take stock of oneself.'

There had been a disturbing mixture of mockery and gravity in the way he had spoken, but she did not linger on this discovery. 'Did you find the trip fruitful in a scientific way?'

'I did,' he confessed, 'but I was also anxious to get back to civilisation.'

'I can imagine,' she murmured, trying to think how she might have felt if she had been in his position.

They drank their coffee, but as the silence lengthened between them Sherry became aware of the nervous tension that had gripped her body since early that morning. She had nothing to fear, she told herself. Rollo had made it quite clear before dinner that evening that his only interest in this marriage was David, but she could not shake off her uneasiness.

'Does anyone in your family, other than your aunt, know about David?'

Her nerves jarred violently as he shattered the silence between them with his query, and she shook her head. 'No.'

His eyebrows rose in mild surprise. 'You never wrote and told them?'

'No.' Her composure was slipping, but she clung desperately to the little that was left. 'The fact that I was unmarried and pregnant was not something I was very proud of.'

His expression hardened. 'You will write to them now, I presume.'

'I might.' She shrugged slightly, and his heavy eyebrows rose once again to meet above his high-bridged nose in a frown.

'Don't you want them to know that you're married, and that you have a child?'

'My mother is too wrapped up in her own marriage to

really be interested, and I can almost say the same for my brother where his career as a doctor is concerned,' she answered casually, placing her empty cup on the tray, but not relaxing her rigid stance on the edge of her chair.

'You have an odd family,' Rollo remarked tersely, adding swiftly, 'with the exception of your aunt in Kromrivier.'

'What about *your* family?' she questioned him, realising that she actually knew very little about him.

'I don't have any,' came the abrupt reply. 'My mother died when I was twelve, and my father lived only long enough to see me through university.'

A compassionate warmth flooded her heart. 'I'm sorry.'

'There's no need for your condolences,' he stated harshly. 'My relationship with my father was a healthy, normal one, just as I intend my relationship to be with David.'

The coldness in his voice sent a chill through her body that lingered there discomfitingly. She was not in a fit state to analyse Rollo, let alone herself. Tiredness was beginning to gnaw at her composure, and she had to stifle a yawn behind her fingers.

'Come on!' Rollo said abruptly, rising to his feet. 'It's time you were in bed.'

Sherry did not argue with him. She *was* tired, too tired to actually feel afraid at that moment, and that in itself was dangerous.

Rollo did not attempt to touch her as they walked up the stairs, but Sherry shrank as close to the balustrade as she could for fear that he might.

'I'll come in with you,' he said when she paused outside the nursery door with the intention of bidding him good night, and she knew she could not refuse him a glimpse of his son before they retired for the night.

David was asleep, lying on his back with his face turned towards them, and his cheeks were rosy in the soft glow of the night lamp. Rollo stared at him in silence for

endless seconds, his emotions hidden behind a rigid
mask, then he leaned over the railings of the cot, and his
strong, sun-browned hand lightly brushed David's dark
curls.

'If I hadn't tracked you down to Kromrivier I would
never have known, would I.'

It was said as a statement, not a query, and it was softly
but harshly spoken not to wake the sleeping child.

'No, you would never have known,' Sherry admitted,
fighting down that stab of guilt which had grown fiercer
these past few days.

'My God!' Rollo grated savagely through his teeth. 'I
could almost kill you for that alone!'

One large hand had been raised as if he had wanted to
throttle her, but his hand dropped to his side again as he
turned on his heel, and strode out of the nursery, going in
the opposite direction to the master bedroom.

CHAPTER EIGHT

SHERRY spent her wedding night in a restless torment on
that four-poster bed in the master bedroom. When the
stars began to fade as a prelude to dawn, it was relief that
drove her from the room and into the nursery, but Connie
had already taken charge of David, and Sherry could not
decide whether she ought to be pleased, or resent it. She
was tired, she admitted to herself, retreating back down
the passage to her own room, and if Connie was looking
after David, then there was time for a refreshing shower
before she went down to breakfast.

She stayed in the shower longer than she had intended,
but it was heavenly to feel the warm water jetting against
her body, and pummelling the tiredness out of her
muscles. Her body felt relaxed when she turned off the
taps and stepped out of the cubicle to towel herself dry.

The wall beside the shower cubicle was a mirror from ceiling to floor, and she paused a moment to study herself critically.

Her grey eyes were larger than usual this morning, with a hint of a shadow circling them. Had she changed much in the physical sense these past two years? she wondered suddenly. Her cheekbones stood out a little more prominently, but the skin that stretched over them was flawless. The wide, full mouth was firmer, less vulnerable, and hard work and exercise had tightened up her body after David's birth. Her breasts were still small and firm, but her hips were slightly fuller.

This marriage would not continue as it had started, Sherry knew that with a frightening certainty. At some future date Rollo would insist upon his rights as her husband, and she would have to submit to him. Would he still find her attractive?

She groaned inwardly and turned away from the mirror to pull the shower cap from her hair. What did it matter what she looked like? Rollo had not married her because he cared; he had married her because she had had his child, and she would do well to remember that. He was claiming a part of David for himself. *David*. A tender warmth softened her eyes and relaxed her tight mouth into a smile. David was her reason for living; from the moment of his birth he had been the axis around which her world had spun, and if she could have her life over again she would make the same choice as before.

She went down to breakfast wearing white cotton slacks and a shirt, with a yellow sash tied about her slender waist. She felt cool and relaxed after her shower, but her body tensed the moment she entered the dining-room. Rollo was seated at the table, and he rose when she approached him. His narrowed glance flicked over her, but his expression remained inscrutable.

'I hope you slept well?' he asked with no real sign of interest as he pulled out a chair for her.

'Yes, thank you,' she answered with frigid politeness,

but her shoulder was caught in a crushing grip before she could sit down, and strong fingers cupped her chin and jerked her face up to his.

'Don't lie to me!' A derisive smile twisted his mouth during his close scrutiny of her raised face. 'Not when the outward signs are there to contradict you.'

The latter had been added almost savagely as he released her, and she subsided weakly into her chair. His touch had unnerved her more than she cared to admit to herself at that moment, but she was also angry.

'All right, so I had a bad night!' she snapped as he resumed his seat at the head of the table.

'That's better.'

'You sound as if it pleases you to know that I didn't sleep well last night,' she accused, her grey eyes stormy with the anger that simmered inside her.

'It *does* please me,' he admitted with that hint of savagery back in his deep voice. 'I spent the entire night thinking of the months I spent in total ignorance in the Antarctic while you carried my child and gave birth to him. If I'd known about him I would have lost no more than six months of his infancy, but instead you deprived me of *fifteen* months. Did you think of *that* last night when you were lying awake?'

Yes, she had thought about that, and she had thought about many other things too, but the blame was not entirely hers. Was it?

'Did you give me any reason to believe you would have liked us to have a future together?' she counter-questioned bitterly. 'You knew how I felt about you at the time, I'd made it disgustingly obvious, and you knew I would have waited for you, but in your letter you were insistent that I find someone else. You didn't *want* me, Rollo. Our relationship was simply a two-week fling before you got on that ship for the Antarctic, and that was where you insisted it should end.' Her throat tightened and she swallowed convulsively. 'I was the besotted fool who'd asked you to stay with me that night, and that's why I accepted sole responsibility for what followed. Can you blame me entirely for not involving you in something you hadn't gone out of your way to encourage?'

'*Dammit*, Sherry!' His fist slammed down on to the table, making everything rattle and bounce precariously, and she jumped nervously. 'I'd always made it a policy never to get involved with a virgin, but you——'

'I know!' she interrupted him, her voice sharp and edged with bitterness, and her face pale. '*I* seduced *you*!'

The telephone rang in the hall during the ensuing silence while they glared at each other, and moments later Bettina entered the dining-room.

'Telephone for you, Professor,' she announced. 'It's Professor Ingram, and he's calling from the SRI.'

Rollo excused himself from the table and strode out of the room, leaving Sherry alone at the table to fight down the bitter rage sweeping through her. Why was Delphine's father calling Rollo from the Scientific Research Institute on the Sunday morning after their wedding? she wondered when she had calmed herself sufficiently. What was so important that it could not wait until the Monday morning?

She lifted the lid of the silver salver on the hot tray. Bacon and eggs. Her stomach tightened with rejection, and she settled for a slice of toast and coffee instead. She could imagine that the beautiful Delphine was not very happy about Rollo marrying someone else. How, Sherry wondered, did Delphine's father feel about it in his position as director of the SRI?

'I'm afraid I have to go out,' Rollo announced when he returned to the dining-room. He poured himself a cup of coffee and drank it without sitting down. 'What I have to do may take all day, so don't expect me home before this evening.'

Sherry sat there at the table long after Rollo had gone. She had taken no more than two bites out of her toast, and the rest of it remained untouched on her plate while

she poured herself a cup of coffee and sipped it slowly.
She could not decide how she felt about Rollo leaving her
alone at Five Oaks. Was she relieved, or did she resent
the fact that he had been called out to the Institute? She
had a nasty suspicion that it was the latter, but she was
not going to admit it. Not even to herself.

Connie brought David to her, and Sherry took him out
on to the lawn in the spacious garden where he played
with his toys until it was time for his morning nap.
Connie was going to be a tremendous help, Sherry could
sense this, and she was grateful for it.

Bettina served tea that morning under the crimson
bougainvillaea which ranked profusely along the pergola
over the slate *stoep* on the east side of the house. Below
the *stoep* a lizard sunned itself contentedly on the low,
stone wall surrounding a shallow fishpond. It was a
sizzling day, and all the signs were there that the weather
was building up to a storm at some future date. Sherry
tried to relax in the shade of the bougainvillaea and,
above all, she tried not to think, but the latter was
impossible in the tranquil silence of that Sunday
morning.

*I'd always made it a policy never to get involved with a
virgin!* Rollo's angry words echoed painfully in her mind.
He had always made it a policy never to get involved with
a virgin, but then she . . . ! Oh, God! *She* was the one who
had begged him to stay with her that night and make love
to her. Rollo had gallantly tried to make her change her
mind, but she had been adamant. She had wanted him;
she had wanted to take the memory of that one night into
the future with her to sustain her, and no man could have
resisted the temptation she had offered. The note he had
left her would forever be seared into her memory. He had
said that he had taken so much from her without giving
anything in return, but he had been wrong. He had given
her David, and she could never have wished for a more
tangible memory to ease the ache in her heart, nor to fill
that void in her soul.

Sherry thrust these thoughts aside and poured herself a second cup of tea which she drank quickly. With Rollo out of the way she had time to explore the house, and when she placed her empty cup on the tray, she went inside and started her exploration on the upper floor.

She discovered that Rollo had slept in a smaller room with an adjoining bathroom which was across the passage from the nursery, and the furniture, although basically plain and simple, consisted once again of well-preserved antiques.

To the right of the stairs there were two furnished bedrooms, a linen-room, and two bathrooms. There was also a guest-room with a bathroom *en suite*. There was sufficient accommodation for several house guests, and she wondered how often this house had been filled to capacity.

Rollo's study was on the ground floor, but Sherry did not venture into it. She went instead into the kitchen, and found it spacious and modern with all the electrical equipment a woman could desire. The staff accepted her presence with politeness and understandable reserve. It would take time for them to accept her as mistress of Five Oaks, just as it was going to take time for her to settle down in her new home.

'What shall I prepare for lunch, madam?' Bettina confronted Sherry before she left the kitchen.

'Something light ... a sandwich, I think,' Sherry suggested hesitantly. 'We can leave the main meal for this evening when the Professor will be home.'

Bettina smiled, obviously approving of the arrangements, and Sherry did not linger to make the kitchen staff more uncomfortable than she sensed they already were.

Sherry was pleasantly surprised when she sat down to lunch that day. Bettina had prepared a plate of tuna sandwiches as one would for a banquet, and, added to that, there was a bowl of mixed fruit on the table with a jug of cold orange juice. Hunger suddenly clawed at

Sherry's stomach, making her realise that she had barely eaten since leaving Kromrivier, and she devoured every single sandwich before helping herself to the fruit.

Rollo returned home late that afternoon when Sherry was bathing David, but she did not see him until she joined him before dinner for a glass of wine in the living-room. He was not in a pleasant mood; she could sense his aggression and his anger, and it made her wonder. Had something happened at the Institute to put him in this foul frame of mind?

'We have one of Germany's leading scientists visiting us at the moment,' Rollo announced after dinner when they were drinking coffee in the living-room. 'Professor Ingram is arranging an elaborate banquet at his home this coming Tuesday evening, and as his assistant I shall have to attend.'

'I don't have to go, do I?' she asked hopefully, but he dashed her hopes at once.

'As my wife you will be expected to accompany me.'

Sherry digested this in silence, and with a certain amount of apprehension. 'I presume Delphine will be there?'

'I have no doubt she will be. Besides being Professor Ingram's daughter, she's also assistant to the head of the research laboratory.'

Sherry tried to gauge his feelings, but his face wore a mask that was impenetrable, and she was forced to voice her uneasy thoughts. 'Won't it be placing you in a difficult and awkward position, having your wife *and* the woman you love under the same roof for the evening?'

Rollo appeared to consider this for a moment, then a faintly sardonic smile curved his sensuous mouth. 'I'll survive the ordeal,' he said. 'The problem is, will you?'

He had flung the ball neatly back into her court, and she answered hastily, 'Yes, of course I shall.'

How silly of her to have been concerned for him when he was so arrogantly self-assured. What had appeared to be a problem to her, was a minor detail to him, and she could almost dislike him for taking it all so calmly while she was beginning to view her immediate future with trepidation, and something else which she did not have time to analyse.

'I'm told it's going to be an elaborate affair, with high-ranking officials listed amongst the guests. Certain members of the press will also be in attendance to cover every facet of Professor Reinhardt's visit to South Africa,' Rollo explained, heightening her apprehension to a plateau of alarm. 'I've opened an account for you at the bank, and I've deposited an amount in it which will be replenished automatically every month. The only thing they still require is your signature, so I suggest you do that first thing in the morning, and spend some time buying yourself an appropriate outfit. I've a small Nissan truck you may use until I've bought you a car to replace the Mini your aunt is selling for you.'

'Thank you,' Sherry murmured stiffly, wishing herself back in Kromrivier. 'You're very kind.'

Rollo's mouth tightened with displeasure. 'Was that meant to be sarcastic?'

'No,' she assured him gravely. 'I'm simply finding it rather difficult accepting the fact that, in future, I shall be dependent on you for what I wear and eat.'

'You'll get used to it.'

'I imagine I shall,' she agreed coldly, sensing a lack of sensitivity which she could not have credited him with two years ago, and somehow it hurt, but she hid her feelings behind a cool, aloof expression. 'If you don't mind, Rollo,' she said, getting to her feet, 'I think I'd like to go to bed.'

'Certainly,' he smiled twistedly, rising from his chair to dominate her with his height, and a gleam of mockery leapt into his heavy-lidded eyes. 'Sleep well.'

Sherry did not answer him. She could not. Her senses had somehow come alive to the familiar scent of his woody masculine cologne, and her pulse was quickening in response to his maleness. It was unfair that he still had

the power to disturb her emotionally, while he felt
nothing at all, and she turned from him rather blindly to
go up to her room before she foolishly allowed him a
glimpse into her treacherous heart.

Sherry was nervous. Her hands were shaking when she
secured the pearl studs in her pierced earlobes, and her
insides felt as if they had coiled themselves into a
permanent, aching knot. She fastened a single string of
pearls about her throat before she stepped back from the
mirror to study the effect, and she had to admit to herself
that her wine-red evening gown added a much-needed
warmth to her pale complexion that evening. What she
needed desperately was confidence in herself and in her
ability to cope with whatever situation might arise that
evening, but outwardly she gave no sign of her painful
uncertainty as she picked up her lacy gold wrap and
evening bag. Rollo would be waiting for her in the living-
room, and she did not want to arouse his anger by
delaying their departure.
   She hurried downstairs, her footsteps muted on the
carpeted floor as she crossed the hall and went into the
living-room. Rollo turned, a glass of whisky in his hand,
and her heart was suddenly beating in her throat. He was
devastatingly handsome in a dark evening suit, and her
trembling limbs refused to carry her forward while his
blue gaze travelled with suffocating slowness from her
glossy hair down to the gold, high-heeled sandals on her
small feet.
   'Do I look presentable?' she questioned him with
concealed nervousness when the silence became
unbearable.
   He put down his glass abruptly and walked towards
her into the prisms of light from the chandelier above
her. Only then did she notice the tension in his facial
muscles, the slight flaring of his nostrils, and the
smouldering fire in his eyes as he continued to subject her
to his intense appraisal.

'I'd forgotten how beautiful you really are, Sherry,' he said throatily, his fingers burning her skin and touching sensitive, receptive little nerves as he trailed them across her cheek and down along her throat to that pulsating hollow at its base.

Sherry trembled inwardly, and parted her lips to draw a careful, steadying breath. There was a dangerous element in the air between them, and the need for self-preservation made her inject a hint of mockery into her voice when she said, 'How very kind of you to say so.'

He stiffened visibly, that stern, inscrutable mask shifting over his face as he withdrew his hand, and the stinging chill of winter was in his eyes when they met hers.

'Let's go, shall we?' he said abruptly, and strode out of the living-room, leaving her to follow him at a near running pace as they stepped out into the night and got into his Rover.

It was a warm night, but Sherry's skin felt cold and slightly damp when she sat stiffly and silently beside Rollo in his car. He was so close to her that she simply had to move her hand slightly to touch him, but there was a mental chasm between them which was so wide that she doubted it could ever be breached. Delphine Ingram also had to be taken into consideration, and Sherry had no intention of forgetting about that. Taking everything into consideration, she was almost convinced that their marriage was doomed before it had actually started. Knowing that Rollo loved Delphine was not going to make it easy for Sherry to accept a physical advance of any nature from Rollo, and making her feelings obvious in this respect would simply drive him farther away from her.

She sighed inwardly as they approached the élite suburb of Bishops Court. Life had suddenly become an arena where they were rushing around in circles without accomplishing anything of importance.

The Ingram mansion was ablaze with lights, and cars

of every expensive make and description were sandwiched in one behind the other along the wide, sweeping
drive. The sound of music and laughter emerged from the
doors and windows which opened out on to the patio, and
Sherry felt her nervousness return like a clawed hand
clutching at her stomach when she got out of the car and
walked in abject silence beside Rollo up the shallow steps
towards the front door.

Professor Ingram and his attractive wife were standing in the magnificent entrance hall of their modern
home to welcome their guests, and their manner towards
Rollo was warm and friendly.

'I'd like you to meet my wife,' Rollo introduced Sherry,
his hand in the hollow of her back propelling her
forward. 'Sherry, this is Professor and Mrs Ingram.'

'Charmed, my dear,' the grey-haired Professor Ingram
smiled somewhat absently, gripping her hand briefly
before he turned away. 'Rollo, there's something I want
to discuss with you.'

He linked his arm through Rollo's and drew him
towards the living-room where the guests gathered and
spilled out on to the patio, and Rollo accompanied him
without so much as a backward glance at Sherry.

'How ungallant of the men to leave us so abruptly!'
Mrs Ingram announced reprovingly, her diamond
necklace sparkling at her throat beneath the overhead
lights, then she smiled ruefully at Sherry. 'You'll find, my
dear, that scientists have little time for pleasantries when
their heads are filled with a scientific project.'

'I imagine you're speaking from experience, Mrs
Ingram,' Sherry smiled, her nervousness evaporating
rapidly beneath the friendly warmth this woman exuded.

'I most certainly am,' Mrs Ingram confirmed with a
mixture of amusement and annoyance. 'Do make
yourself at home, Sherry, and I hope you enjoy yourself.'

'Thank you,' murmured Sherry, making her own way
into the living-room as Mrs Ingram turned to welcome a
party of people who had just arrived.

Delphine might have her mother's looks, Sherry decided, but she lacked her mother's obvious warmth and charm, and that was such a pity.

The music, bordering on the classical and pleasant on the ear, was supplied by a four-piece band at the far end of the enormous living-room, and people were milling about, standing almost shoulder to shoulder as they sampled the snacks and helped themselves to drinks at the bar. To Sherry it seemed as if she had stepped into a fashion house of expensive jewellery and elaborately designed evening gowns.

She cast an interested but wary glance about her. She was surrounded by people, some of whom she had seen photographs of in the newspapers, but she had never felt more lonely. She caught sight of Rollo across the crowded room. He was standing in an alcove beside a potted palm, and he was talking to Professor Ingram and a lean, slightly stooped man with wild grey hair and bushy grey eyebrows and moustache. Sherry was tempted to join Rollo, but she did not want her action to be misconstrued and, above all, she did not want to intrude on what appeared to be a grave scientific confrontation.

She stood about idly, not quite knowing what to do with herself, and feeling conspicuous. 'Follow the stream,' she eventually told herself and, picking up a plate, she helped herself to the cold buffet supper which had been laid out on the tables close to her. She had never felt more awkward, but she suspected that this was how Rollo had intended her to feel, and it angered her.

Sherry ate very little. The food seemed to lodge in her throat, and it felt as if a million eyes were focused on her when she approached the bar and asked for a glass of wine with which to ease that tightness in her throat. She was attended to swiftly, and shrank back into the crowd milling about.

Where was Delphine?

The thought had barely crossed her mind when she turned to see Delphine making her way towards her in a black, shimmering evening-gown which appeared to be moulded to her shapely body.

'Well, hello there,' Delphine greeted her with a smile, but her grey-green eyes were cold and critical as she looked her up and down. 'I must say I notice a vast improvement since the last time we met, but then you didn't have Rollo's bank account to back you up.'

'All the more reason for me to enjoy it now, wouldn't you say?' Sherry retaliated swiftly to the deliberate insult, but she almost regretted it the next instant when Delphine's lovely features became faintly distorted with hatred and fury.

'Your clever little scheme may have worked to trap Rollo into marrying you, but don't revel too much in your success!' Delphine hissed. 'Rollo isn't a fool, and I doubt if it will take him long to discover that he isn't the father of your child.'

'If that's what you're hoping for, then you're going to be disappointed,' Sherry parried this vicious attack with a calmness she was far from experiencing.

'We shall see,' Delphine smiled twistedly, recovering her composure with a visible effort. 'Enjoy the rest of your evening, darling.'

Sherry was shaking inwardly when Delphine spun away from her. She had never before met a woman who could be so beautiful and yet so obnoxious, and it amazed her that she could be the daughter of the pleasant couple who had welcomed Rollo and herself at the door earlier that evening.

'I wouldn't be surprised if that young lady pours venom over her breakfast cereal every morning,' a laconic male voice remarked behind Sherry when she was swallowing down the remainder of her wine in an attempt to steady herself, and she almost choked on the fiery liquid as she spun round to find herself face to face with a stocky young man whose brown eyes were on a level with hers.

'You heard?' she asked warily, wondering frantically

how many other people had heard Delphine's hateful and humiliating remarks.

'I couldn't avoid hearing,' he smiled almost apologetically. 'I was standing directly behind you when the young lady launched her attack, and she has a voice that carries a little beyond the person she's addressing.'

'It was her deliberate intention to embarrass me,' Sherry voiced her opinion, glancing about her surreptitiously, and discovering to her relief that no one was looking her way.

'You're not going to let her succeed, are you?'

'Not if I can help it!' she answered determinedly, concentrating once again on the young man with the faintly sallow complexion.

'Good girl!' he grinned, his glance appreciative as it flicked over her. 'The name's Samuel Hutton, by the way, and my friends call me Sam.'

'Sherry Jae—van Cleef,' she corrected herself hastily as she introduced herself.

'Van Cleef,' he repeated thoughtfully, then his expression cleared. 'Ah, then that must be your husband standing there chatting to Professors Reinhardt and Ingram, and ... Oh, dear, the venomous lady isn't wasting time, is she?' Sherry followed the direction of his gaze to see Delphine joining the three men in the alcove across the room, and there was something distinctly possessive in the way she linked her arm through Rollo's. 'She's making a public bid for your husband, and she doesn't care who knows it,' Sam Hutton added with a measure of distaste in his voice.

Sherry was engulfed by a searing stab of jealousy. There was absolutely no sense in denying it, but she refused to acknowledge the reason for it.

'Are you also a scientist?' She hastily changed the subject, focusing her attention on the man beside her who was still frowning in the direction of the alcove across the room.

'Do I look like a scientist?' he counter-questioned, his

eyebrows raised in amusement.

'I haven't associated with scientists long enough to notice whether they all bear a specific trademark relating to their profession.' She forced her stiff lips into a smile while she studied Sam Hutton intently. 'If you're not a scientist, then what are you?'

'I'm a journalist,' he confessed with a slightly twisted smile. 'Professor Reinhardt is news, and that's what my paper wants.'

She regarded him with renewed interest, 'I always imagined that journalists never went without a camera slung about their necks, and a notebook and pencil in their hands.'

'One notebook and pencil,' he announced with a grin, producing them from the jacket pocket of his evening suit, 'but, alas, no camera. The photographic side of this assignment is being taken care of by that clever young lad who, at this moment, is taking photographs of Professor Reinhardt and company, and the venomous lady is making very sure you won't be the one to appear in the morning papers with your husband.'

Sherry had not needed to be informed of that fact. Her glance had strayed in that direction a second earlier to see the young photographer aiming his camera at the group in the alcove, and she had felt again that searing stab of jealousy when she saw Delphine arrange her shapely body in a provocative pose against Rollo's tall frame a fraction of a second before the flash of the camera immortalised the moment.

Her features were controlled when she turned once again to face Sam Hutton. 'I hope you're not going to add this personal drama into your account of the proceedings this evening?'

'I'm your friend, lady, not your enemy,' he told her with an injured look on his face. 'And I have a strong arm for you to lean on if you should need it.'

Sam Hutton's sincerity could not be denied. He was undeniably a professional man with integrity, not a news-hungry reporter clutching at anything and everything that came his way, and Sherry relaxed.

'Thank you,' she smiled, the tension easing out of her at last. 'I should have known that you were not that kind of journalist.'

'Let me get you a drink,' he suggested, his grin infectious, and she did not object when he took her arm and guided her towards the bar.

She no longer felt like an awkward outcast with Sam Hutton at her side. He was someone to talk to, someone to fill the void of Rollo's neglect, and she would be eternally grateful to this man for his moral support.

Sherry did not have an opportunity to speak to Mrs Ingram again, but she did catch a glimpse of her several times during the course of the evening as she mingled amongst her fifty or more guests. She was a graceful, charming hostess, but her daughter was something else altogether.

It was almost two hours after their arrival at the Ingram home that evening that Rollo put in an appearance at Sherry's side, and her anger rose by several degrees when her sensitive nose detected Delphine's perfume clinging to his evening suit.

'It's time we went home,' he said blandly, making no attempt to apologise for his neglect, and she felt her blood pressure rising by several degrees.

'I'm ready whenever you are,' she said coolly, but they were detained before they had taken a pace towards the door.

Delphine appeared at his side and, ignoring Sherry, clasped Rollo's arm with both her manicured hands. 'Darling, do come with me. Daddy would like you to meet a man who's very interested to discuss your findings on the Antarctic.'

The Antarctic! Damn the Antarctic! Sherry hated the very name. Rollo's trip to that frozen part of the world had flung her into a life of misery which had been lightened only by the birth of their son, but the misery, she knew, was bound to linger on.

Rollo seemed to hesitate for a fraction of a second, his mouth tightening almost as if he had sensed the thoughts coursing through Sherry's mind, but the next instant he had excused himself, and was allowing Delphine to lead him away across the room.

'Alone again?' a now familiar voice demanded some minutes later, and Sherry turned with a faintly cynical smile on her lips to face Sam Hutton.

'So it seems,' she observed wryly, accepting a glass of wine from him which she had not wanted, but which she felt she needed at that moment. 'I'm beginning to think I should have stayed at home.'

'That would have been a disaster,' he smiled, adding softly, 'for me.'

Sherry returned his smile over the rim of her glass as she took a sip of wine, then her expression sobered. 'You've been very kind this evening, and I can't thank you enough.'

'It was no chore keeping company with a lovely lady like yourself,' he brushed aside her remark, 'and, if it will be of some slight consolation to you, I've asked the photographer to scrap that photograph with the venomous blonde in it.'

She was speechless for a moment. Kindness was not something one ought to expect from a member of the press. That, at least, was what she had always been led to believe, but Sam Hutton was obviously an exception to the rule. He had a heart, and a keen perception which must have told him how much she had dreaded the thought of enountering that photograph in the daily newspaper.

'You're a remarkable man,' she said gravely, deeply touched by his kindness.

'I'm a sucker for a pretty face,' he contradicted her, but she knew this was not the truth.

She let it pass, however, when she saw Rollo approaching her with a look of barely concealed disapproval on his ruggedly handsome face. Sam Hutton had seen him as well, and he raised his glass to Sherry in a final salute.

'Perhaps we'll meet again some time,' he said, then he melted away among a group of men crowding around the bar.

Rollo's expression was enigmatic when he joined her, but there was a piercing quality in the narrowed eyes that met hers. 'Let's get out of here.'

Sherry did not like his tone of voice, but this was not the time to protest, and she hastily disposed of her glass to accompany him out of the house. It was a calm, star-studded night, but she had an uneasy feeling that a storm was brewing which had nothing to do with the weather.

CHAPTER NINE

THE silence in the car during that drive from the Ingram mansion to Five Oaks had been anything but companionable, and Sherry was relieved when Rollo allowed her to enter the house while he garaged the Rover. Connie met her in the hall to assure her that David had not awakened once, and Sherry thanked her before she hurried up the stairs to her room.

She switched on the bedside light, undressing quickly and slipping into her nightgown and her old, wide-sleeved silk robe before brushing her teeth, and creaming off her make-up. She tried to shake off that uneasy feeling that a storm was about to break loose over her head, but it persisted while she brushed her hair vigorously.

Her glance fell on a slim volume of poetry in her dressing-table drawer when she dropped her brush into it. It was her favourite book of poetry, and when she took it out it fell open at a page marked with a photograph

taken two years ago of Rollo and herself in the cable car
ascending Table Mountain. She was smiling in the
photograph, happy simply to be with him, and his arm
was draped lightly about her shoulders while he smiled
down at her. She had looked at that photograph so many
times during the past two years, and her feelings had
ranged from pain to numb acceptance of what she had
considered no more than a dream. Now the pain was
back again, and her glance shifted to the short,
anonymous poem she had underlined once with a pencil.

> Stay, O sweet, and do not rise!
> The light that shines comes from thine eyes!
> The day breaks not: it is my heart,
> Because that you and I must part.
> Stay! or else my joys will die
> And perish in their infancy.

Those words had summed up her thoughts and her
feelings very accurately during those last few hours they
had shared together before he had left for the Antarctic.
Did she still feel that way?

The sound of footsteps in the passage made her start,
and she hastily returned the volume of poems to the
drawer before she twisted round on the dressing-table
stool to see Rollo entering her room and closing the door
behind him. Why the sight of him should alarm her she
could not imagine. Since her arrival at Five Oaks he had
made a practice of visiting the nursery each evening
before retiring, and he usually looked in on her briefly
before going to his own room, but he had always been
fully dressed before, whereas now he was wearing a blue
towelling robe with the deep vee down the front exposing
far too much of his powerful, sun-browned chest for
comfort.

Sherry rose to her feet, that uneasy feeling spiralling
inside her as his stormy gaze drew hers across the room.
He thrust his hands into the pockets of his robe, and

there was something dangerous in the set of his wide shoulders.

'What did that reporter chap want?' he demanded harshly, and her body stiffened with annoyance.

'He's not a reporter, he's a journalist.'

'What did he want?' Rollo repeated his query, ignoring her remark.

'Nothing,' she snapped, turning from him to tighten the lid of her bottle of cleansing lotion unnecessarily.

'Nothing?' he laughed harshly, appearing in the mirror behind her, and there was something frighteningly sinister about his rugged features in the dimly lit room. 'He spent the best part of the evening with you, and you say he wanted nothing?'

Alarm bells rang in her mind, warning her to exercise care, and she forced herself to say calmly, 'I'm tired, Rollo, and this discussion isn't important.'

That was the wrong thing to say, she knew it the moment the words left her lips. His eyes narrowed, and his mouth tightened with an anger she was beginning to feel as if it were her own.

'It's important to me when I know that people were speculating about my wife spending almost the entire evening in the company of another man,' he announced gratingly, and Sherry was momentarily taken aback, but she rallied swiftly.

'If they were speculating about me, then they must also have been speculating about you.'

'What do you mean by that?' he snarled, a whiteness settling about his nose and mouth that gave him a terrifying appearance, but she was suddenly too angry to solicit caution.

'Oh, for God's sake!' Her anger had been simmering all evening, but now it erupted, and she was shaking as she spun round to face him, her eyes blazing up into his. 'You dumped me the minute we arrived at the Ingram house this evening, and the rest of the time you had Delphine hanging all over you!'

The silence that followed her outburst was almost deafening, and there was a stillness about Rollo which once again gave her that odd feeling that this was the calm before the storm.

'Delphine joined us without an invitation from me,' he said at length, 'and you could have done the same.'

Was there a rebuke in his voice, or did she imagine it? 'I was under the impression that you were having a private, scientific discussion with Professor Reinhardt, and I didn't want to intrude.'

'We did have a brief discussion of that nature,' he confirmed, 'but you could have joined us later.'

Oh, he was very clever, Sherry had to acknowledge that. He had spun the situation around very neatly to lay the blame on her, and perhaps she *was* partly to blame, but not without reason.

'I'm new to this world you live in, Rollo, and I'm not quite sure what's expected of me as your . . . wife.' She felt her colour coming and going as she faced him, but she pressed on. 'If I was free to join you, then you could have indicated the fact to me in some way instead of leaving me to think that I'd be in the way.'

'I don't think you particularly wanted to join us,' he accused bitingly. 'I think you were enjoying that reporter chap's company too much to be bothered with anyone else.'

'As a matter of fact I did enjoy his company,' she retaliated sarcastically. 'Just as much, I'm sure, as you enjoyed Delphine's.'

'I suggest we leave Delphine out of this.'

Sherry paled as if he had struck her, and she brushed past him to open the bedroom door. 'Good night, Rollo.'

Her heart was thudding as he walked towards the door. She would not rest until he had gone, but she discovered, to her dismay, that he had no intention of leaving. The door was removed from her clasp, and closed firmly once again. Her heartbeat quickened to a suffocating pace, and fear sent its first icy darts through her body when she noticed the resolute set of his square jaw with that suggestion of a dimple she remembered so well.

'You mentioned the fact that you were my wife,' he said, an ominous ring to his voice, 'and I think it's about time you started behaving like my wife.'

Her face went a shade paler as she stared up at him. She knew what he was referring to, but there was a part of her that refused to accept it. 'What—what are you talking about?'

'I'm talking about the fact that we're married,' he smiled twistedly. 'It's time our marriage settled down to normality.'

'You're not thinking of—of——' She faltered, uncertain all at once, and she backed away from him. 'Rollo, you wouldn't!'

'Why shouldn't I take what I have a legal right to?' he demanded, his rugged features ruthless in the dim light of the bedside light.

'Because it isn't *me* you want, it's *Delphine*, and I won't be used as a substitute!' she argued desperately.

'Oh, I wouldn't say you'd be a substitute,' he smiled mockingly, his glance sliding down the length of her in a way that made her feel as if he was mentally stripping her down to her skin, and her body became heated with embarrassment. 'You're beautiful; beautiful enough to have made that reporter chap run circles around you all evening, but I happen to have the advantage of being your husband, and I also happen to know that we can be pretty damn good together in bed.'

'No!' she almost screamed at him, shrinking away from his touch for fear that he might defile the memory of something which had once been beautiful between them. 'Stay away from me!'

His hands shot out, gripping her shoulders in a painful vice that forced her to bite down hard on her lower lip to prevent herself from crying out, and she was pulled up against him with a savage force that almost drove the breath from her body.

'You didn't behave like an outraged virgin two years ago,' he mocked her ruthlessly. 'Why behave like one now?'

'Two years ago you weren't in love with Delphine,' she defended herself, fighting against the mental and physical wounds he was inflicting, and fighting also against the fear that her treacherous body might betray her.

'I said we'd leave Delphine out of this!' he warned, flames of anger leaping in his eyes.

'We can't!' she cried, desperate to escape from a situation which was too humiliating to contemplate. 'Do you think there's a woman on this earth who would enjoy being made love to by a man while knowing that he was thinking of someone else at the time?'

'I think you've misunderstood me.' Her shoulders were freed from the painful grip of his hands, but her attempt to escape was foiled. His arm was like a steel band about her waist while his free hand grasped a handful of golden-brown hair, and her head was jerked back, forcing her pale face out into the open. 'I shan't be thinking of anyone else while I'm making love to you, Sherry. You're beautiful enough to make me forget,' he explained mockingly, his ruggedly handsome face so close to hers that she could feel his warm breath against her mouth.

'Oh, God!' she groaned, closing her eyes, and forcing back the tears that threatened to spill from her lashes.

Of all the times her heart could have revealed the truth to her, this was the worst. *She loved Rollo!* She had never stopped loving him, and she would go on loving him no matter how often, or how deeply, he chose to hurt her.

Her hands were tightly clenched against his chest, her body taut with resistance, but pleasure mingled with alarm when she felt his warm mouth against her exposed throat, seeking and finding those incredibly sensitive areas to send tiny darts of pleasure stabbing through her. She tried to push him away from her, knowing that if she

allowed him to continue she would be lost, but her
strength was puny against his, and there was no escape
from that sensuous mouth when it finally took possession
of hers. She tried desperately not to respond, but he
coaxed her lips apart, and a surging tide of warmth
flowed through her body, releasing it from its self-
confined prison.

Sherry's resistance crumbled like a house of cards. For
one frantic moment she thought of Delphine, then
everything else was forgotten except the fire he was
kindling inside her. Her fingers uncurled against his
chest, and her treacherous body melted against his rock-
hard frame. She was trembling, craving his touch
suddenly like an addict in desperate need of a shot in the
arm, and shivers of pleasure coursed through her when
his hand slid down from her hair into the opening of her
robe to stroke her breast.

'I want you, Sherry,' he murmured huskily against her
mouth, his fingers teasing the hardened peak of her
breast until it ached with desire. 'God knows, I've never
stopped wanting you.'

Her mind screamed out in protest. He wanted her, but
he did not love her. If only she had the strength to resist
him, but that aching longing pulsating through her body
robbed her of her pride, and she did not resist when
Rollo's impatient hands tugged at the belt of her robe and
slid it off her shoulders. Her nightgown followed, sliding
down along her slender body to join her robe on the floor,
and then she was lifted in his arms and carried towards
the enormous four-poster bed. He lowered her on to it,
his fiery gaze devouring her while he discarded his
towelling robe, and she closed her eyes, praying for that
breath of sanity which might save her from certain
humiliation, but it continued to evade her.

She felt the bed sag beneath Rollo's weight, and knew
it was too late. Their bodies touched, her feminine
softness yielding against his hard, masculine frame, and
then his lips and hands commenced their devastating

exploration, igniting fires she had almost forgotten during the past two years. The urgency of his intimate caresses aroused a searing hunger deep down inside her, and her desire rose swiftly to match his. A little gasp of surrender escaped her, and she arched her body towards his, urging him with her hands on his lean, hard hips to fill that aching void inside her.

Their union was silent, but stormy and passionate, and there was no room for anything or anyone else. There was only a driving need for the physical satisfaction of the flesh, and when it was over, Sherry lay spent in his arms, but she was not content. She had made love with her body, but her mind and her soul had remained untouched. Perhaps the fear of being hurt had made her subconsciously withhold that part of her that mattered, and it left her feeling sick inside. Two years ago she had held nothing back when they had made love. It had been a beautiful, almost sacred experience, but what she had done now shocked her rational mind and made her feel as if it had been something sordid.

Tears filled her eyes and ran slowly down her cheeks when Rollo switched off the bedside light and sighed deeply beside her. He was asleep almost at once, but Sherry was awake for some time yet, trying desperately to halt the silent tears. Her pillow was drenched with those hot, stinging tears that scalded her cheeks, and she felt drained when at last they stopped.

Sherry had been awake most of the night. She was too aware of Rollo in the bed beside her, and of his arm and his leg weighing her down inescapably when he flung them across her in his sleep. Exhaustion finally claimed her in the early hours of the morning, but she was awake again at five, and relieved to find herself alone.

She knew she would not sleep again, she was too disturbed even to try, and she got up, pulling on her robe which Rollo must have picked up off the floor and thrown across the foot of the bed before he left. She went into the bathroom to run her bath water. Her body was aching as if she had taken physical punishment, and she longed for a relaxing soak in the hot scented water.

Half an hour had elapsed before she finally got out of the bath. She wrapped a bath sheet around her, and when she caught sight of herself in the wall mirror she realised that the crumpled sheets and pillows on the bed were not the only signs that Rollo had spent the night with her. The skin on her shoulders had discoloured where his fingers had bitten so painfully into her flesh, and it felt tender to the touch.

Damn Rollo! *Damn* him for what he had done to her, and to the memory she had cherished for so long! She could not ignore her own part in it, and shame sent the blood surging into her pale cheeks as she cringed inwardly at the memory of her willing surrender the night before.

She went down to breakfast two hours later with her bruises carefully concealed beneath the short sleeves of her grey and white striped cotton frock. She had steeled herself to confront Rollo, but there was no one in the dining-room when she entered it and seated herself at the table. Scrambled eggs and bacon were being kept warm on the hot tray, but the thought of food made Sherry feel ill, and she helped herself to a cup of coffee instead in the hope of steadying those quivering nerves at the pit of her stomach.

She had the time to compose herself to some extent, but that did not prevent her heart from leaping wildly in her breast when Rollo walked into the dining-room a few minutes later. He looked so vital, and so totally relaxed and refreshed in his beige lightweight suit that she could almost hate him for the dreadful way she felt.

'Good morning,' he said, his voice cool and polite, and Sherry responded in an equally cool, polite manner as he seated himself at the head of the table and helped himself to scrambled eggs and bacon.

She was not quite sure what she had expected, but she

had not been prepared for his chilly remoteness. At the very least she had expected to be mocked and ridiculed, but nothing like that happened. He ate his breakfast in silence as he had done every morning since their arrival at Five Oaks, and it was as if nothing had happened the night before. If she had not had the bruises to show for it, then she might have been able to convince herself that she had had a nightmare, but the memory of that beautifully proportioned male body moving against her own in that primitive rhythm of desire was still too fresh to discard so lightly.

What was she to make of this? she wondered, pouring herself a second cup of coffee with a hand that shook slightly. She ought to feel relieved, or perhaps annoyed, but she felt neither. She merely experienced a deep-seated anguish at the knowledge that she had been used once again. She meant no more to him than the beautiful *objets d'art* scattered throughout his home. The only difference was that he had not hesitated to use her, and he would use her again without compunction.

'I'd like you to arrange a dinner party for a week on Friday.' Rollo at last broke the silence between them, pushing his plate aside and helping himself to a cup of coffee. 'You may invite Jonathan and Brenda, and I'd like to invite a young colleague of mine, Peter Grundlingh, and his wife. I'd also like to invite Professor and Mrs Ingram.'

'Will your invitation to the Ingrams include Delphine?' she asked, holding her breath mentally.

'Naturally.' His impersonal glance flicked over her. 'You wouldn't want me to exclude Delphine, would you?'

'No, of course not,' she answered stiffly, clamping down on that fierce stab of pain that shot through her. 'Would seven-thirty on the Friday evening be a suitable time, do you think?'

'That would be perfect.' He drained his cup and rose from the table. 'Don't wait dinner for me this evening, I shall be late.'

He strode out of the dining-room, leaving Sherry with the feeling that a lead weight had settled in her breast. She heard him drive away in his Rover, and she wanted to cry when some of the tension eased out of her, but this time she resisted that self-pitying desire.

So Rollo wanted her to arrange a dinner party to which he was going to invite Delphine. Well, if he could invite that venomous creature, then she could also invite whom she pleased, and, with that thought in mind, she left the table and walked into the hall. She looked up the telephone number of the newspaper where Sam Hutton worked, and punched out the number on the telephone with an agitated finger.

It took a minute or two before she was put through to Sam Hutton, and he recognised her voice immediately. 'Lady, this must be telepathy,' he said, his voice pleasant and warm. 'I was actually thinking about you when the telephone rang.'

'Were you?' she asked a little doubtfully, wondering if she actually had the courage to go through with what she had in mind.

'I was wondering if I would see you again, and when.'

'What about dinner here at Five Oaks a week on Friday?' She issued the invitation before she could change her mind, and Sam whistled softly at the other end.

'I don't think your husband will like that very much.'

'My husband is going to invite Delphine Ingram, and I don't happen to like *that* very much,' she confessed. 'I was hoping you would come along and give me the moral support I know I'm going to need. Will you come?'

'I'm a regular Sir Galahad, so count me in,' he laughed. 'I've never been able to resist a lady in distress, and I also happen to want to see you again.'

'Thank you, Sam,' she sighed, feeling a little guilty about the fact that she was using him in this way.

'By the way,' Sam Hutton interrupted her disturbing thoughts, 'we worked almost through the night to get that article on Professor Reinhardt into this morning's edition of our newspaper, so I suggest you go out and get a copy. There's a lovely photograph of you and your husband arriving at the Ingram mansion last night, and it ought to make a certain young lady green with envy!'

Sherry could not prevent the laughter that spilled from her lips, but she wondered some time afterwards whether she ought to have found it so amusing. Delphine Ingram might be a 'venomous lady', as Sam Hutton had dubbed her, but she was still human. If she loved Rollo, then that photograph could hurt her as much as it would have hurt Sherry to see the photograph of Rollo and Delphine in print.

Her hand was still resting on the telephone receiver. She had a second call to make, and she was hesitant about it. She had married Rollo in such confusion and haste that she had neglected to contact Brenda, and Brenda would have every right to be hurt and annoyed at the knowledge that she had been left in ignorance. There was, however, no sense in delaying the inevitable, and she lifted the receiver to punch out Brenda's number.

The telephone rang for a considerable length of time, and Sherry was about to replace the receiver when a familiar, and rather breathless, voice sounded in her ear.

'Brenda Hunt speaking.'

'Brenda, it's Sherry, and I know you're going to be angry with me,' she began apologetically.

'You're damned right, I'm angry!' Brenda exploded. 'I open the newspaper this morning, and what do I see? Professor and *Mrs* van Cleef arriving at a posh banquet arranged for Germany's Professor Reinhardt. My God, why didn't you let me know?'

'There wasn't time,' Sherry explained lamely, 'and, quite frankly, I was in such a mental turmoil about my marriage to Rollo that I could hardly think straight.'

'When am I going to see you?' 'Today, I hope,' Sherry replied. 'Do you think you could meet me for lunch at the open-air restaurant in the Gardens?'

'What time?' Brenda queried abruptly.

'What about twelve-thirty?'

'I'll see you then,' said Brenda, 'and you had better tell me everything in the minutest detail, or I shall never forgive you.'

'I'll tell you everything,' Sherry promised. 'I know I owe it to you.'

She replaced the receiver a moment later with a sigh of relief. It hadn't been so bad after all, and she was looking forward to having lunch with Brenda. She had to get out of the house, the walls were beginning to close in on her, but she would not have contemplated it if she had not known that David would be quite happy about being left in Connie's care.

Sherry arrived early for her luncheon appointment with Brenda, and she chose a table beneath a large tree, with an unpronounceable botanical name, which cast dappled shade on to the checkered tablecloth. She had bought the newspaper, and she paged through it while she waited. The photograph of Rollo and herself was indeed a good one. She could not recall the photographer taking it, but he had certainly caught them in a pose which would have allowed no one to guess at the stress and tension in their marriage. She was still reading Sam Hutton's interesting article which accompanied the selection of photographs, when a shadow fell across the newspaper, and she looked up to see Brenda glowering down at her.

'Well? And what have you got to say for yourself?' Brenda demanded, looking down her nose at Sherry.

'Sit down, Brenda,' Sherry instructed, suppressing the desire to smile. 'You look and sound exactly like Matron Naudé at the moment.'

'God forbid!' snorted Brenda, pulling out a chair and lowering herself into it, but her expression remained indignant and angry. 'Well, are you going to give me all the disgusting details, or aren't you?'

'After we've ordered lunch,' Sherry insisted, indicating to the waitress that they were ready to order.

'How typical!' Brenda snorted again somewhat disdainfully. 'You always did enjoy evading the issue and leaving me in suspense.'

'I never had breakfast this morning, and I do happen to be starving,' Sherry defended herself.

'Very well, let's order,' Brenda sighed resignedly as the waitress paused beside their table with her pencil poised over her order pad. 'I dare say I shall succeed in restraining my curiosity until after we've eaten.'

Brenda's aggression was short-lived. It was not in her nature to remain angry with anyone for longer than five minutes if she could help it, and this, coupled with her patience, would have made of her an excellent nurse if she had not loved her wild, late-night parties more.

They ate their salad lunch in comparative silence, and Sherry poured their tea before she explained briefly what had occurred since the last time they had met, ending with Sam Hutton's kindness to her during the function at the Ingram residence the previous evening.

Brenda lapsed into a thoughtful silence, her hazel eyes intent on Sherry's face which bore the unmistakable signs of her sleepless night and what had occurred to induce it.

'Do you still love him?' she asked eventually, and the suddenness of her query stripped Sherry of the ability to be evasive.

'Yes,' she answered simply.

'And Rollo?'

Sherry gestured helplessly with her hands. 'He's never denied that he's in love with Delphine, and that he would have married her if he hadn't known about David.'

'He's never denied it when you have confronted him with it, but he's never actually said so, has he?'

'No.' Sherry stared at Brenda. It was quite true. She was the one who had been the first to mention the touchy subject of his love for Delphine, and he had not denied it. Neither had he denied her allegations that he had wanted to marry Delphine. Was it possible that . . .? *No!* She shook herself free of that thought. 'Don't make me hope, Brenda,' she said reproachfully, 'because I don't honestly believe I have anything to hope for.'

'I know there were rumours that he was planning to marry Delphine,' Brenda continued undaunted, 'but I've always had the feeling that it was one-sided.'

'You mean Delphine wanted to marry *him*, and not the other way around?'

'Exactly!' Brenda nodded. 'Delphine latched on to him the moment he stepped ashore ten months ago, and Rollo has always been a man who knew what he wanted and made sure that he got it in a hurry. Don't you think he would have married her long ago if that's what he had really wanted?'

Sherry did not know what to think. What Brenda was saying made beautiful sense, and she wanted very much to believe it, but she dared not.

'This is all pure conjecture, and it will lead us nowhere,' Sherry brushed aside the matter, and hastily changed the subject. 'Are you and Jonathan free a week on Friday in the evening?'

'I believe we are. Why?'

'I'm inviting you to dinner at Five Oaks, and I hope that seven-thirty will suit both you and Jonathan.' Sherry gripped her hands together in her lap until her fingers went numb. 'Professor Ingram and his wife will be there, and one other couple, Peter Grundlingh and his wife. Rollo is also going to invite Delphine.'

'Oh?' Brenda's eyebrows rose a fraction in surprise. 'I imagine you're not exactly ecstatic about that.'

'No,' Sherry admitted, a faintly cynical smile curving her soft, generous mouth, 'but I've retaliated by inviting Sam Hutton, the journalist I told you about.'

Amusement danced in Brenda's hazel eyes, but it was gone the next instant to leave her features grave. 'Something urges me to warn you that you're playing a dangerous game.'

'Maybe I am,' Sherry acknowledged defiantly, 'but I'm not going to have Delphine crawling all over Rollo while I sit back meekly and suffer the humiliation.'

'And what about Sam Hutton?' Brenda touched a sensitive area that once again aroused a feeling of guilt. 'The man has obviously discovered he has a soft spot for you, and I wonder if you've stopped to consider that you might hurt him as well as yourself in the process.'

Sherry had given this a great deal of thought since she had telephoned Sam Hutton so rashly that morning, and it troubled her, but she was desperate.

'What would *you* have done under the circumstances?' she challenged, seeking from Brenda an alternative to this hopeless and near desperate situation in which she had become entangled.

Brenda considered this for a moment, then she sighed and raised her hands helplessly in the air. 'I guess I would have done exactly the same as you're doing now.'

Sherry smiled wryly, and gestured to the waitress to order a fresh pot of tea. Sharing her problems with Brenda might not have solved anything, but it had lightened the load, and it had left her with something to think about. Was it possible that she was wrong about Rollo being in love with Delphine? Even if this was true, her logical mind warned, it did not alter the fact that Rollo had asked her to marry him because she had had his child, and she had agreed mainly because of her fear of losing David.

CHAPTER TEN

SHERRY had dinner alone that evening, but she felt restless and agitated. A dreadful suspicion had taken shape in her mind to quell that faint flicker of hope Brenda's remarks had lit in her heart earlier that day.

Was Rollo working late at the SRI, or was he with Delphine?

She tried to curb her thoughts, but her mind continued on its relentless path of destruction and torment, and she went up to her room after dinner with a mixture of desolation and rage sweeping through her. She was beginning to think she had been a fool to marry Rollo, but it was too late now to bewail the fact. She had walked into this agonising trap with her eyes open. She knew now that it had not been her fear of losing David that had made her agree to marry Rollo. She had agreed because, deep down, she had known that she still loved him, and the agony she was suffering at the moment was the price she had to pay for loving so unwisely. If she had sent Rollo away she might eventually have settled down to a contented, if not entirely happy, marriage with Gordon Shaw.

God, what was she thinking about? She could never have married Gordon loving Rollo the way she did. She would never have succeeded in making Gordon happy and, no matter how much she might have tried, Gordon would always have known that he was second best. He deserved better than that from the woman he married, and she hoped fervently that he *would* marry someone nice, someone who would love him as he deserved to be loved.

Sherry sighed deeply. She had made her choice, and she would have to live with it for the rest of her life. There would be no divorce. This was a stipulation Rollo had made on the eve of their wedding, and she had agreed, but she had never imagined the depth of the mental agony she would suffer at the knowledge that she was married to a man who did not love her.

She was in bed late in the evening when she heard Rollo's car crunching up the gravel drive, and her hand made an involuntary movement towards the bedside light to switch it off, but she realised in time that it would be futile to pretend that she was asleep. Rollo would have noticed that her bedroom light was still on, and he would merely mock her attempts at trying to avoid him.

Her hands tightened on the book she had been trying to read, and she stared at it fiercely, but the words danced before her eyes without making any sense. She could hear Rollo's heavy but muted footsteps in the passage, and her heart was beating so hard and fast in her throat that it almost cut off her breath. He went into the nursery, she could hear his step on that uncarpeted section of the floor in the passage, and her body was suddenly so tense that she would have snapped if she had been a twig.

Her bedroom door opened a few minutes later, and out of the corner of her eye she saw Rollo entering and closing the door quietly behind him. He took off his jacket and his tie, and flung them across the armchair. He was unbuttoning his shirt almost to the waist as he walked towards her, and she shifted the position of her legs slightly when he sat down on the bed beside her. Only then did she raise her glance from the book in her hands to find herself looking up into tired blue eyes, and her tension and anger was forgotten for the moment.

There was nothing about him to suggest that he had spent the past few hours in another woman's arms. He had, instead, the look of a man who was pushing himself so hard in his profession that his health could be endangered, and her tender, caring heart melted with concern.

'I must say it's quite a novel experience arriving home and finding my wife waiting up for me,' he announced, that hateful gleam of mockery entering his tired eyes.

'Don't flatter yourself, Rollo!' she snapped, her compassion fleeing to make room for anger and disappointment. 'I'm awake for the simple reason that I've been reading.'

He glanced at the historical novel she was clutching in her hands, and his mockery deepened. 'It can't be a very interesting book if you've been reading all evening and you're still on page three.'

She snapped the book shut and glared at him. 'I've had other things on my mind.'

'Such as?' he prompted with a twisted smile.

'I had lunch in town with Brenda today,' she told him. 'She's accepted our invitation to dinner.'

'And so has everyone else I suggested this morning.'

'Including Delphine?' she asked warily.

'Yes, including Delphine,' he dashed her fragile hopes, his expression shuttered as he rose to his feet. 'I'm going to have a shower.'

He was pulling off his shirt as he walked, his back muscles rippling beneath his tanned skin, and her eyes widened at the direction he had taken. 'That's *my* bathroom!' she protested agitatedly.

'From now on it's *our* bathroom,' he corrected, turning his dark head to glance at her over his shoulder, and even at a distance his sensuous appraisal made the blood flow a little faster through her veins. 'I shan't be long.'

His knowing smile made her cringe with embarrassment. He knew exactly what he was doing to her, and he was enjoying it. *Damn him!*

'You can take all night for all I care!' she stormed at him, her grey eyes blazing, but the only answer she received was his deep-throated laughter when he entered the white-tiled bathroom and closed the door behind him.

Sherry sat there fuming while she listened to him whistling off-key in the shower, but she was beginning to direct her anger at herself. If only she could hate him instead of loving him and wanting him so much! And if only she wasn't so transparent about the way she felt!

There was no sense in attempting to escape the inevitable. It would only make her look as ridiculous as she was feeling at that moment, and a renewed burst of his derisive mockery was something she could do without. She opened her book, pretending to read and trying to appear relaxed when she heard the shower taps being turned off, but her body was tense, and her taut nerves jarred at every little sound.

The bathroom door opened seconds later, and all her good intentions to appear cool and relaxed were shattered. She looked up from her book, the first fatal mistake, and she found herself staring almost hypnotically at that magnificent male body with the towel draped carelessly about his lean hips.

Rollo's dark hair lay in damp disarray across his broad forehead, giving him a slightly boyish appearance that appealed to her senses. Their eyes met, the second fatal mistake, and somewhere deep inside her a quivering warmth erupted and swelled until it swamped her completely.

The bed sagged beneath his weight when he sat down beside her, drops of moisture still glistening on his wide shoulders when he removed the book from her hands and flung it aside. The clean male smell of him was more potent than a drug, and her heart was racing so fast that her breathing was impaired. A flame had been lit in his eyes, and it was slowly devouring her, lingering on the sheen of her hair, her delicate, flushed features, and the clamouring pulse at the base of her throat.

The tips of his fingers brushed lightly against the bruises on her shoulders, and his touch sent a thousand little pleasure darts shooting through her, but it was nothing compared to the sensations he aroused when he lowered his head to trail his warm, sensual mouth across the bruises he had inflicted the night before.

'Don't, Rollo!' she pleaded huskily, her mind still clear enough to reject what her treacherous body was responding to so deliriously, and Rollo raised his dark head to consume her with eyes in which the flame of desire was now burning fiercely.

'I want you, Sherry,' he murmured, his deep, vibrant voice tearing at her swiftly crumbling resistance. 'I had a pile of work waiting for me this morning, and I've had an agonising day trying to wade through it when all I could think of was the way you felt in my arms.'

How effortlessly you transfer your desire from one woman to another, she wanted to say, but the words were stilled on her parted lips when the lacy straps of her nightgown were slid off her shoulders to expose her breasts to the sensually erotic exploration of his heated mouth.

Her eyelids felt heavy, and she lowered them until her lashes veiled eyes that had become dark and languorous with her mounting desire. She lifted her arms, shrugging herself out of the bodice of her nightgown at the same time, and it was Rollo's hands that pulled the flimsy material down to her waist while she slid her hands across his smooth shoulders until her fingers became locked in his dark, damp hair.

It no longer mattered that he did not love her; she had enough love for both of them and, God help her, she wanted him so much that she simply did not care. If this was all she could have of him, then she would have to resign herself to it, and pray that in time he might learn to care a little.

Rollo lifted her from her reclining position against the pillows, and draped her over his arms while his fiery mouth trailed yet another destructive path along the sensitive areas of her throat to her eager, parted lips. He kissed her with a sensual hunger that heightened her arousal, and the abrasiveness of his chest hair against her breasts added to her mounting excitement.

'God, Sherry, it's good to feel you against me like this,' he groaned against her mouth, 'but I want to feel every part of your beautiful body against mine.'

What am I doing? she asked herself, the last flicker of sanity invading her drugged mind when her slender softness was crushed against the hard length of Rollo's body. Do I have no shame, or self-respect left? How can I let him do this to me when I know that, in his heart, it's Delphine he wants?

Her body stiffened with resistance, but the intimacy of his stroking fingers ignited an aching fire inside her. The shutters of her conscious mind slammed shut, and her body arched towards his with an invitation he did not ignore.

Rollo's breathing was ragged during their tempestuous lovemaking, and those little whimpering cries could only have come from her own lips, Sherry realised, when they lay entwined in each other's arms, shuddering in the aftermath of their passion. But she was consumed with shame after that euphoric feeling had dwindled.

'What's the matter?' asked Rollo when she freed herself from his arms and turned her back on him.

'Nothing!' she snapped, choking back her tears and shrugging off his hand. 'Just leave me alone!'

'I'll leave you alone, if that's what you want,' he sighed angrily, switching off the light. 'God knows, I've had a long day, and I'm too tired right now to deal with a temperamental woman.'

Temperamental! How dare he accuse her of being temperamental! Her shame was forgotten in the wave of anger that swept through her. He was an insensitive, arrogant . . .! Oh, God, she was going to cry, and she turned her face into the pillow to stifle the sound.

Sherry began to dread the nights, knowing that her inevitable surrender would leave her fighting a silent battle against that overwhelming sense of shame, and as the weekend approached she began to show visible signs of those sleepless hours each night when her mind would give her no peace.

They had not planned anything for the weekend, and Sherry had wondered how she was going to survive during those two days, but she was surprised at how calmly and pleasantly the time passed. Rollo was courteous and attentive, and she could almost make herself believe he enjoyed spending time with David and herself.

The weather was unusually hot on the Sunday, and it seemed to sap her energy to the extent that, when she put

David down for his afternoon nap, she decided to rest for an hour as well. She had not intended to sleep, but she did, and she awoke with a start two hours later.

David was not in his cot when she entered the nursery, but she was not alarmed until she went downstairs and met Connie entering the house from the side *stoep* ... without David!

'I've laid out a tray of tea on the *stoep*, madam,' she enlightened Sherry. 'It's cooler there than inside the house at the moment.'

'Thank you,' Sherry murmured absently. 'Where is David?'

'The Professor took him into the garden.'

Sherry's eyes widened. She could not decide whether she ought to feel relieved or anxious as she walked quickly out of the house. She did not have to search far. Rollo had taken David into a shady nook in the spacious, well-kept garden. He had spread out a blanket on the green lawn, and he was seated on it with David's toys surrounding them.

She paused beneath an archway along which small crimson roses ranked profusely, and she watched with bated breath when David raised himself unsteadily to his feet and toddled on his chubby legs towards Rollo to collapse with a gurgling laugh in his father's arms. Rollo's deep-throated laugh made Sherry expel the air slowly from her lungs, but the look on Rollo's face, when he hugged his son against his breast, brought a lump to her throat which she had difficulty in swallowing down.

Love and guilt did not blend well together, and it took some moments for her to compose herself before she made her presence known. 'It's time to have tea,' she said interrupting their game reluctantly.

Rollo looked up, the warmth in his eyes intended for the little boy who stood on wavery legs clutching at his father's shirt, but, for a brief second, some of that warmth spilled on to Sherry before his cool, polite mask shifted back into place.

She felt weak and shaky when she walked beside Rollo who was carrying David on his arm, and when they reached the *stoep* her desire to weep was almost stronger than her desire to pour their tea and pretend that nothing was wrong, but she dared not let Rollo see how strongly she had been affected by what she had seen.

The agonies of her personal relationship with her husband were not the only things that afforded her sleepless nights. She had begun to realise that she had behaved much too rashly when she had issued that spur-of-the-moment invitation to Sam Hutton. Jealousy had prompted her uncharacteristic action, but knowing this did not salve her stricken conscience and, worst of all, she did not know what to do about it.

After a moderately calm weekend, the Monday started on a more relaxed note, and Sherry was lulled into believing that, whatever Rollo's feelings for Delphine, their marriage did have a chance to succeed. This foolish assumption was shattered that very same day. They were having coffee in the living-room after dinner that evening when the telephone rang, and Sherry gestured to Rollo to remain seated while she went into the hall to answer it.

'I'd like to speak to Rollo, if it isn't too much trouble for you to call him.'

Delphine Ingram's musical voice had the sting of a viper in it, and Sherry had difficulty in controlling the wave of anger that swept through her.

'It's no trouble at all,' she assured Delphine with a calmness she had dredged from somewhere and, placing the receiver on the circular rosewood table, she returned to the living-room and resumed her seat. 'It's Delphine,' she answered in response to the curious glance Rollo directed at her, 'and she wants to speak to you.'

Rollo raised a quizzical eyebrow, but he rose at once and went into the hall. 'Hello, Delphine,' Sherry heard his voice quite clearly. 'Now?' he questioned after a brief pause, and there was a second lengthy silence before he added an abrupt, 'Very well.'

Sherry was sitting rigidly in her chair when Rollo returned to the living-room. She knew what he was going to say, and she did not want him to say it, but there was no way that she could stop him.

'I have to go out.'

'So I've gathered,' she retorted icily, 'but if you must have an affair with Delphine on the sideline, then you could at least be more discreet about it.'

The only reaction she received from Rollo was the slight clenching of his hands at his sides and a narrowing of his eyes. 'I'll bear that in mind.'

Her face whitened when he strode out of the house and left her with the feeling that she had received a crushing blow where it hurt most.

She drew a ragged, tortured breath as she heard Rollo drive away and, almost blinded by a near physical pain, she went up to her room and closed the door behind her to lean against it with her eyes closed. It was incredible that she could love a man who had no qualms whatsoever about hurting her like this. Delphine simply had to call, and he dropped everything to go to her.

'Oh, God!' she groaned, choking back the tears that threatened. 'How am I going to bear it?'

She pushed herself away from the door and went into the bathroom. Her mind was her worst enemy at that moment. It was conjuring up cruel visions of Delphine in Rollo's arms, kissing, making love and . . . God help her, she could not stand it!

She bathed and got into bed. She tried to read, but she found herself staring blankly at the pages. Her mind was filled with thoughts of Rollo and Delphine, and they tormented her to the extent that beads of perspiration broke out on her pale forehead.

It was long after ten o'clock that evening when Sherry heard Rollo entering their darkened bedroom. Her body tensed, and her heartbeats escalated to a thundering pace which she prayed silently he would not hear while he moved about in the darkened room and undressed himself. If he touched her tonight she would be physically ill, she thought, while she lay there pretending to be asleep, but she need not have feared this. Rollo got into bed beside her without touching her, and it seemed as if mere seconds had elapsed before she realised that he was asleep.

Her fury at that moment very nearly overshadowed her pain. Did he have no conscience at all? How could he go to sleep with such apparent ease while his actions had ripped at her soul like the claws of a savage lion? I could kill him at this moment for doing this to me! she thought with equal savagery, but as the night wore on she found relief only in the silent tears she eventually shed into her pillow.

Sherry was on her way down from the nursery on the Wednesday morning when the doorbell chimed. She was expecting Brenda to call on her that afternoon, but no one else had made an appointment to see her that day, and her smooth brow creased in a slight frown as she crossed the hall to open the door.

Sam Hutton stood there, a faintly apologetic smile curving his thin mouth? 'May I come in?'

'Yes, please do,' she said hastily, recovering from her surprise and opening the door wider for him to step inside. 'You've arrived in time for tea,' she added as she led the way into the living-room, and she silently blessed Bettina for her habit of preparing tea for three or more, even though Sherry was usually the only one there to drink it.

'Very nice,' Sam Hutton remarked, glancing about him with genuine appreciation. 'Very nice indeed.'

Sherry was feeling extraordinarily tense when she gestured him into a chair and seated herself on the sofa behind the tray of tea which had been placed on the low, marble-topped table.

'Do you take milk?'

'Yes, please,' he nodded, watching her pour their tea with a hand that was not quite steady. 'I hope you don't mind my dropping in unexpectedly like this, but I'm afraid I'm going to have to disappoint you.'

'In what way?' she asked, holding her breath mentally as she passed him his cup of tea.

'I'm being sent on an assignment to Port Elizabeth, and I shan't be here on Friday evening to give you my moral support.'

Relief washed over her at his disclosure, but it did not eliminate that feeling of guilt which had dogged her this past week, and she knew she would not be able to live with herself until she had cleared her conscience completely.

'I understand,' she assured him gravely. 'Actually, Sam, I owe you an apology. I was going to use you shamelessly, and I've been feeling extremely guilty about it. I've also spent this past week trying to think of a way to rectify the situation without hurting you.'

'You don't have to apologise,' he laughed away her discomfort. 'I did offer my services, remember?'

'I know,' she nodded, 'but that isn't sufficient excuse for my rash behaviour.'

'Forget it,' he instructed, drinking his tea thirstily while Sherry sipped at hers. 'Has the problem been sorted out?'

'No,' she answered quietly and with grim honesty.

'I see.' He leaned back in his chair and studied her intently for a moment. 'Will you consider taking advice from me as a journalist who has witnessed and lived through more traumas than I care to remember?'

'Quite honestly, Sam, I'm at a stage now where I would take advice from the garbage remover if he cared to offer it,' she laughed shakily.

'Well, my advice to you is this,' he said, leaning forward as if to stress the importance of the advice he was about to give her. 'Don't be so hesitant and retiring. If you want your man, then go out and get him. Fight for him, if you have to, and use the advantage you have of being his wife.'

Sherry considered his advice gravely, but she shrank inwardly at the thought of what it would entail. What would Rollo think if she suddenly took a possessive stand where he was concerned?

'I know what you mean,' she smiled wanly, 'but I don't know if I'm capable of following your advice.'

'Of course you are!' Sam contradicted firmly, but with a glimmer of amusement lurking in his brown eyes. 'And I wish I could be a fly on the wall Friday evening to observe and applaud you.'

Sherry was not convinced that she would be capable of giving a performance worth applauding, but she knew that his advice was worth considering.

'More tea, Sam?' she offered.

'No, thanks, I must be off,' he said, getting to his feet. 'I'll give you a call some time when I get back.'

'Do that,' she smiled, accompanying him to the door. 'And thank you . . . for everything.'

'You can thank me if you have followed my advice and if it worked,' he grinned at her, raising his hand in salute and going quickly down the shallow steps to his blue Mazda parked beneath a shady tree in the drive.

She went inside when he had driven away, and poured herself a second cup of tea which she drank without actually being aware of what she was doing. Did she have the courage to take his advice? She had never lacked courage before, but this was somehow different, and Rollo might not find it amusing to have his wife taking a stand against the woman he loved. Could she risk it? Dared she?

CHAPTER ELEVEN

THE dinner party on the Friday evening started off without any major hitches. Peter Grundlingh and his wife, Joyce, were a pleasant couple with whom Sherry had no difficulty in communicating. Mrs Ingram was her charming, gracious self, while her husband, a brilliant scientist according to Rollo, appeared to be rather absentminded at times, but Delphine's haughty manner gave Sherry all the indication she needed that the evening would not pass without a few sparks flying between them. And then, of course, there was Brenda and Jonathan Hunt without whom, Sherry was forced to admit, the party would have been a rather dull affair.

Delphine was wearing emerald green that evening, but once again it was a clinging creation that left nothing to the imagination. *Vulgar exhibitionism* would have been Aunt Margaret's old-fashioned opinion, and Sherry would have been inclined to agree with her. The men, however, found her physically appealing and, for a time, Rollo appeared to be incapable of taking his eyes off her.

Sherry, however, had no need to feel inferior. Her full-length evening dress was the colour of rich cream, and there was a touch of gold in the lacy sash about her slender waist, while the soft folds of the long skirt swayed about her legs when she got up to go and check on the dinner preparations.

Brenda rose and followed her swiftly from the living-room, and they had barely entered the hall when Brenda demanded in an angry hiss, 'What does that bitch think she's doing?'

Sherry did not need to be told that Brenda was referring to Delphine Ingram, but 'bitch' was not quite the word Sherry would have used to describe that woman. 'Vampire' suited her best, Sherry decided, recalling the way Delphine had clung to Rollo's arm while smiling coyly up into his face, and since her arrival she had dropped the word 'darling' all over the place as if she had been afraid it might go out of fashion.

'Rollo invited her,' Sherry said in answer to Brenda's query as they approached the kitchen, 'and he obviously approves of her behaviour.'

'The man must be out of his mind!' Brenda exploded, her lovely face almost distorted with fury.

'Or genuinely besotted with the woman,' Sherry responded, thrusting that savage sword deeper into her wounded soul while she hid her own anger behind a practised mask of calmness.

Brenda snorted disparagingly when they entered the kitchen, but they had to cease their conversation in front of the staff.

Sherry sat facing Rollo across the long length of the dinner table during the evening. Their guests had been arranged on either side of the table, but somehow Delphine had managed to rearrange the seating to place herself at Rollo's left. This intensified Sherry's anger, but she remained silent, and with her smile intact.

The kitchen staff had excelled themselves, and everyone was complimentary . . . except Delphine. To no one in particular, she said, 'I imagine the staff must find it rather unpleasant having to take orders from a strange woman when they've had a free rein here at Five Oaks for such a long time.'

If you want your man, then go out and get him, Sam Hutton's voice leapt into Sherry's mind to prompt her. *Fight for him, if you have to, and use the advantage you have of being his wife.*

'I can't say I've noticed any displeasure amongst them.' Sherry's soft, controlled voice carried into the brief, uncomfortable silence which had developed around the table. 'They have, on the contrary, been very kind and considerate in helping me to settle down here.'

'Perhaps that's because Rollo has always paid them so well.' Delphine smiled beguilingly at Rollo, her slender, manicured hand stroking his black-clad arm.

'And perhaps it's because I haven't thrust my authority on them in a way that could offend,' retaliated Sherry, succeeding at last in capturing Rollo's blue gaze across the length of the table. 'Wouldn't you say that's the case . . . *darling*?' She added the latter in a syrupy tone for good measure.

Amusement mingled with the mockery glittering in his eyes. 'I would say you're probably right, my dear.'

Delphine did not like the endearment Rollo had tagged on to his reply, and her grey-green eyes flashed fiery dislike at Sherry.

'You must be very proud of your son, Rollo.' Brenda touched on a subject which was sure to infuriate Delphine. 'I came to tea the day before yesterday, and I couldn't help noticing that David is the absolute image of you.'

Rollo smiled, and accepted Brenda's remark with a slight inclination of his dark head, but, before he could say anything, Delphine leapt in with, 'You must find it extraordinarily tedious with a child in the house crying and keeping you awake at night.'

Heads were beginning to turn from left to right like spectators at a tennis match when Sherry responded to Delphine's remark.

'David has actually been an angel, and he hasn't disturbed us once during the night.' Sherry was surprised to discover that she was actually beginning to enjoy herself, and she smiled provocatively at Rollo. 'Isn't that so, darling?'

He raised a heavy eyebrow in sardonic amusement, but he did not let her down. 'I can't say I've heard him in the night, and I'm a very light sleeper.'

Grey-green eyes were shooting daggers at Sherry once again, and heads were swinging from left to right as if to determine from which side the next round would be fired, but it was Delphine's mother who graciously entered the arena in a somewhat belated attempt to save the inflammable situation.

'I believe you're a qualified nurse, Sherry.'

'A qualified nursing *Sister*, Mrs Ingram,' corrected Brenda, chipping in before Sherry could formulate a reply. 'And she's a damned good one too.'

'Thanks for the compliment, Brenda,' Sherry said, trying to brush aside her friend's remark, 'but my qualifications are insignificant when you stop to consider that we have no fewer than three scientists and an engineer seated around this table.'

'Did you rule the lives of the young nurses like a tyrant?' Peter Grundlingh questioned Sherry humorously, his fair head tilted slightly in her direction while he waited for her to reply.

'No, I didn't,' she said at once. 'At least, I don't think I did,' she added after a momentary pause for thought.

'You don't seem very sure,' Peter teased.

'I always found the nurses under my supervision an orderly and disciplined group of girls,' she explained. 'We all got along very well.'

'I've always had difficulty in picturing you as a stern disciplinarian, Sherry,' drawled Rollo, drawing her glance across the length of the table and holding it compellingly.

'I had to be stern sometimes, it was part of my job,' she smiled at him, aware that everyone's eyes were suddenly focused on her. 'You're a scientist, Rollo, and I'm sure that, in your position, there've been occasions when you've had to take stern disciplinary actions.'

'If that's a query, then you'll have to direct it at Peter,' he mockingly flung the ball into someone else's court, and Sherry dragged her gaze from Rollo's to direct it at the fair-haired man on her left.

'Is my husband a stern disciplinarian at times?' she questioned him.

'He is,' Peter admitted readily, 'but he's also a fair one.'

'Yes,' Sherry smiled, a hint of cynicism curving her generous mouth when she met Rollo's compelling gaze at the other end of the table once again. 'You've always been fair, haven't you, darling?'

This was a two-way communication which was crackling as if with static electricity. She had made a veiled accusation which had nothing to do with his disciplinary abilities as assistant director of the SRI, and the slight narrowing of his eyes told her that he was not unaware of this.

'I doubt if I've always been fair,' he smiled twistedly. 'People make mistakes, and I'm not infallible.'

Was that a confession? An apology, perhaps? Her probing glance left her none the wiser, and she sighed inwardly as she placed her table napkin on the table beside her empty dessert plate.

'Shall we have our coffee in the living-room?' she asked, pushing back her chair to rise gracefully to her feet, and everyone agreed. Professor Ingram also emerged abruptly from his reverie to grunt his approval.

'May I use your downstairs cloakroom?' Delphine asked Sherry when they stepped into the hall.

'Certainly,' Sherry answered, her voice cool but polite. 'Do you know the way?'

Delphine adopted a 'little-girl-lost' look. 'Well, I . . .'

'If you'll come this way, then I'll show you,' Sherry offered. 'I practically have to pass it on my way to the kitchen.'

'Thank you,' Delphine smiled with a sweetness that placed Sherry instantly on her guard.

What's she up to? Sherry wondered as Delphine fell into step beside her. The flags of battle were still flying high in Delphine's eyes despite the smile on her crimson lips, and Sherry was not fooled for one instant. Her guard was up, and it would stay there.

'You'll find the cloakroom at the end of this short

passage.' Sherry indicated the direction Delphine had to take, but she knew somehow that this was not going to happen.

'Don't be an idiot!' Delphine sneered, her grey-green eyes glittering with fury. 'You know damn well that I pretended not to know the way so I could speak to you alone.'

'So, here we are, and we're alone.' Sherry's voice was calm despite the turmoil raging inside her. 'What is it you wanted to speak to me about?'

'Don't think I'm not aware of the silly game you've been playing all evening, but you might as well know that it won't get you anywhere.' Delphine was so self-assured, so confident, that it actually frightened Sherry. 'Rollo loves *me*! He may be married to you, but it's *me* he'll return to again and again, because we belong, and because no one can appreciate his scientific mind the way I do.'

It was only Sherry's years of training as a nurse that helped her to keep a firm grip on her control at that moment, and her voice was cool and outwardly unaffected when she asked, 'What makes you so sure that Rollo loves you?'

'Isn't the fact that I'm here this evening proof enough for you, darling?' Delphine demanded with that smug self-assurance Sherry was beginning to hate.

'I'm afraid not,' Sherry persisted, continuing the act she had started at the dinner table, and which she knew she would have to carry through to the bitter end that evening.

'Very well,' Delphine smiled venomously. 'I shall simply have to see to it that you receive further, more consequential proof, and perhaps then you will drop this act of "domestic bliss", which may have fooled the others, but it hasn't fooled me, and neither does Rollo find it particularly amusing.'

'I don't know if you're aware of this, but Rollo made a stipulation before our marriage that there would be no divorce.' Sherry played the only card she had in her possession. 'Would you please explain to me what satisfaction you'll derive out of a relationship with a man who is married to someone else, and who intends to remain so?'

'I think I know Rollo better than you do,' Delphine laughed derisively. 'He married you because he felt obliged to do so and, no matter what stipulation he might have made, the yoke he put around his own neck is going to become far too heavy a burden for him, and he'll leave you . . . for *me*!'

'Don't be too sure of yourself,' warned Sherry, ending this distasteful confrontation by walking away from Delphine and entering the kitchen.

She was shaking when she closed the door behind her, and she felt like ice despite the warmth in the kitchen. Delphine's remarks had struck home with a certain amount of truth, and if Sherry had won the battle at the dinner table, then this round was very definitely Delphine's.

Sherry suddenly became aware of Connie and Bettina observing her curiously, and she pulled herself together quickly to smile at them. 'The dinner was superb,' she complimented them, 'and we're ready to have coffee in the living-room.'

'Are you not feeling well, madam?' asked Connie, her dark eyes mirroring concern. 'You were very pale when you came into the kitchen.'

'It's a slight attack of indigestion,' Sherry lied. 'I ate too much at dinner, and now I'm suffering for it.'

The evening wore on endlessly, but somehow Sherry succeeded in projecting that image of calm hospitality despite Delphine's cloying, sickeningly sweet behaviour, and the fact that Rollo did not appear to object.

Sherry was, however, intensely relieved when everyone left, and she sagged physically and mentally when she reached her bedroom. She had been married for a brief two weeks, but it felt as if she had lived a lifetime in which she had aged considerably.

She had undressed herself, and she was sitting listlessly on her side of the bed when Rollo entered the room and started taking off his clothes. Tired as she was, she was aware of his powerful masculine attraction, and her heart began to beat a little faster. She did not want to look at him, but he sat down beside her, stripped down to his underpants, and his strong fingers turned her face towards his and tilted it up for his inspection.

'Well . . . *darling*?' he mocked her, making her cringe inwardly with shame. 'Your performance as the doting wife was very convincing this evening, so let's see how convincing you can be now that we're alone.'

Sherry did not have the strength to resist him when his mouth settled on hers with a somewhat brutal passion that seared her to the very core of her being. She went limp against his hard male body as he shifted her higher up on to the bed, bearing her down on to it with his weight, and she hated herself for her helpless response to the fiery delight aroused by the intimacy of his stroking fingers.

She surrendered without resistance, following where he led, but a part of her remained detached as if it could not bear to be associated with what she was allowing.

'Not bad,' Rollo remarked caustically when his desire for her had been sated, 'but this performance of yours could have done with a little more warmth.'

If Rollo had struck her physically it would have been less painful, and she smothered her anguished gasp in the pillow. He had obviously wanted to hurt her, and he had succeeded by making her feel like a cheap slut who had received payment for something which had given displeasure. She had, perhaps, deserved some form of punishment for her behaviour that evening, but not this . . . not *this*!

It was like rubbing salt into a raw wound when Rollo got up out of bed, took his clothes with him, and spent the rest of the night in the room opposite the nursery.

Sherry cried herself to sleep that night. She wept choking tears that racked her body and left her feeling oddly drained, and totally exhausted.

Rollo did not come to her room again during the ensuing days and, although he was always polite and courteous, his manner was so distant that the chasm between them had widened to a point where she was convinced it would never be breached. They had not been married quite three weeks, and they had reached a crisis stage. Like a patient caught in the grip of a destructive fever, this was the turning point, and no one, least of all Sherry, could predict the outcome.

The telephone rang at five-thirty on the Thursday afternoon of the following week. It was Rollo, and Sherry felt her heart leap into her throat at the sound of his voice.

'I'm going to be home late this evening, so don't wait dinner for me,' he told her in that cool, distant manner that cut her to the quick.

'Shall I ask Bettina to keep something in the oven for you?'

He seemed to hesitate a moment before answering her. 'If you wish.'

'Very well ... and, Rollo,' she added hastily, afraid that he might ring off and break this fragile contact which she needed so desperately, 'thanks for letting me know.'

The line was silent for several heart-stopping seconds, then he said abruptly, 'Give David a good night kiss for me.'

Sherry put down the receiver with the feeling that the crisis had not yet veered one way or the other, and she was still feeling that way half an hour later when the telephone rang once again.

'Hello, Sherry,' Delphine's melodious voice came across the line. 'Did Rollo let you know that he would be working late this evening?'

'Yes, he did,' Sherry confirmed, a coldness invading her body which she could not understand.

'Well, he lied to you,' Delphine announced triumphantly. 'I'm expecting him here to my flat any minute now, and if you want proof of this, then you're welcome to drop in, but I somehow doubt that you're the type of wife who would want to embarrass herself as well as her husband by storming in on him when he's with another woman.' This was the turning point in the crisis, and the direction it took could not have left Sherry feeling more shattered had Rollo's gabled home caved in on top of her.

'Thank you for the information, Delphine,' she heard herself say with a voice so icily calm that she could not believe it was her own. 'Was there anything else?'

'I should imagine that what I've told you is quite enough,' Delphine laughed derisively. 'Enjoy your evening alone, darling.'

Enjoy your evening alone! Those words screamed through Sherry's mind, tearing at her sanity until she wanted to crawl into a hole somewhere and howl like a wounded animal.

Delphine was smarter than Sherry had imagined. She had promised consequential proof, and she had delivered it. Was there anything left to salvage between Rollo and herself?

Sherry felt a numbness setting in that blanked out the pain which was crucifying her. She would feel again tomorrow perhaps, but not now. Not now!

The nightmare had not yet ended for Sherry. She was crossing the hall at six-thirty that evening to sit down to her solitary meal in the dining-room when the front door opened and Rollo walked in. She stared at him as if she was seeing a ghost, and her tortured mind was suddenly flung into a mad confusion. If he was supposed to be with Delphine, then what was he doing here? She wondered if she was hallucinating, but hallucinations did not speak, she realised, when Rollo's deep voice penetrated the loud soaring in her ears.

'We hit a snag on one of our projects, but the problem was sorted out much quicker than I'd anticipated.' He lowered his head suddenly to peer intently into her white face. 'Are you feeling ill?'

She shook her head, partly in answer, and partly to clear it, then she turned away from his prying eyes. 'You're just in time for dinner.'

'Good!' he said abruptly, following her into the dining-room.

Sherry could not eat. Her mind was racing in mad never-ending circles, and the food lodged nauseatingly in her throat. What are they trying to do to me? she wondered frantically when the pain returned to gnaw away at her. Delphine was waiting for him in her flat. Why had he not gone to her? What had made him change his mind? Why had he come home?

She was confused to the extent that her head felt dizzy, and she did not linger in the living-room that evening after she had had her coffee.

'I'd like to have an early night,' she excused herself, and she escaped without waiting for Rollo to reply.

She went up the stairs, her hand clutching at the wooden balustrade for support, and her heart thudding heavily in her breast. Her mind was still grasping and discarding everything that had occurred during the past two hours, and she was beginning to feel exhausted with the effort to try to understand. Nothing made sense, and she was not in a fit state to question Rollo without making her own feelings humiliatingly obvious.

She went into the bathroom to run her bath water, and stripped off her clothes without actually being aware of what she was doing. She pushed her hair into her shower cap and soaked herself for almost half an hour in the warm, scented water before she soaped herself. She was beginning to feel slightly better, less fragile, and when she stepped out of the bath a few minutes later she dried herself vigorously with the towel until her skin tingled. She took off her shower cap, letting her hair fall free to her shoulders, and she was reaching for her nightgown when the bathroom door opened unexpectedly. Startled almost out of her wits, she grabbed the towel since it was closest to her, and held it up against her body for protection, but not before Rollo's razor-sharp glance had caught a glimpse of nicely rounded hips and firm, pointed breasts.

She had never thought to lock the door against him, but she wished now that she had. After his leaving her to sleep alone for almost a week in that enormous bed she considered this a flagrant invasion of her privacy, but her heart was beating with something other than anger in her throat as she stood there staring at him through the steamy haze between them.

Barefoot and without a shirt, he was exuding a powerful aura of raw masculinity, and the assault on her senses was violent. His blue briefs hugged his lean hips, exposing his long muscular legs, and her breath locked in her throat when she finally raised her glance to his. She knew why he was there, she could read him almost like a book at that moment while his eyes burned their sensuous way down the length of her, and her body was suddenly trembling in response.

'No!' she croaked desperately, shaking her head when he approached her slowly in the steam-filled bathroom. 'No, Rollo. I don't . . . *No!*'

He paused less than a pace away from her, and his eyes blazed down into hers until it felt as if he wanted to probe her soul. The air was pregnant with almost pagan emotions, and past and present suddenly came together with a force that held her immobile. His hands circled her waist behind the towel she clutched in front of her, his strong fingers spread out, cool against her warm, damp skin, and his touch set a thousand little nerves quivering with something close to expectancy. Sherry despised herself, but she had somehow lost the will to resist, and she made no attempt to stop him when he lowered his head to touch his lips to the sensitive skin against her smooth shoulder.

'You smell nice,' he murmured throatily, his mouth trailing a light, fiery path towards her throat, and shivers of delight rippled through her to leave her weak and receptive.

Her mind was still whirling in utter confusion, but her lips were parting to welcome the sensual exploration of her mouth. She was alive, she was his woman, and she had never wanted him more than at that moment. Only Rollo could make her feel this way; only Rollo could make her come alive to her needs as a woman, and she yielded physically and mentally to the sensations he was arousing.

Sensing her surrender, he lifted her in his arms as if she was a child, and carried her into the bedroom. He lowered her carefully on to her feet beside the bed, and only then did he take his mouth from hers.

'You don't need this,' he said thickly, removing the towel she had clutched against her, and then she was lifted on to the bed.

His mouth ravaged hers, and his hands roamed her body in tantalising caresses to ensure her complete surrender. Only then did he leave her side to divest himself of his blue briefs.

'I want you,' he groaned, feasting his eyes on her slender, shapely body as he lowered himself on to the bed beside her. 'For two long years I have wanted you, and I shall go on wanting you.'

What was he saying? What was he talking about? Her mind was ready to spin into ever-increasing circles of confusion, but Rollo's hungry mouth sought hers with a white-hot passion that wiped out everything that had gone before. He made love to her this time with an almost agonising slowness, his fingers stroking her intimately and arousing her to a fever pitch where she begged him to take her.

'We have all night, *liewe meisie*,' he laughed softly and triumphantly, touching her soul with that half-forgotten endearment, and she could almost hate him for the ease with which he seemed to control his own desire.

Their lovemaking was prolonged, erotic and exciting, but in the end her pleasure was so intense that she cried out with the force of it, and clung to Rollo's shuddering body as wave after wave of the most exquisite sensations surged through her.

'*Liewe meisie,*' Rollo groaned that familiar endearment into her silky hair spread out across the pillow. 'You might as well accept the fact that I'm never going to let you go out of my life again.'

Sherry did not say anything. She was emotionally too spent to speak, and physically too beautifully sated to want to think about anything other than what they had shared. Later, perhaps, she would think rationally again, but not yet.

'Will you stay with me, Sherry?' he asked eventually when they lay quietly and relaxed in each other's arms.

She did not want to face the reality, but he was forcing it upon her, and she sighed as she got up out of bed and put on her robe. That gnawing pain was tearing at her insides again when she tightened the belt about her waist and walked towards the window.

'What about Delphine?' she asked, pulling aside the curtains and staring down into the moonlit garden.

'To hell with Delphine!' he exclaimed harshly. 'I'm talking about us. You and me!'

'We can't talk about *us* until we've talked about *Delphine*,' she insisted, drawing the curtains across the window again and turning to find Rollo sitting up in bed with the sheet barely covering the lower half of his magnificent body. Her love for him was a living, throbbing thing inside her, but she dared not let him know it ... not yet ... and perhaps never! 'You love Delphine, and you were going to marry her,' she reminded him, thrusting that painful sword deeper still into her own heart.

'I think it's time I set the record straight,' he said

grimly. 'I have *never* been in love with Delphine, and I have *never* had the slightest desire to marry her. God only knows where you picked up that crazy notion, but I was angry enough with you at the time to let you go on believing it.'

Sherry stared at him, incredulous disbelief mirrored in her grey eyes. 'You're not in love with her?'

'I never have been, and never will be,' he insisted firmly.

'When you went to her flat the other night...' She paused, shaking her head in bewilderment.

'She said she had something urgent to discuss with me, and she didn't want to talk about it on the telephone,' he explained with a hint of anger in his deep voice. 'When I arrived at her flat she was in a slightly hysterical state, and she was going on about some idiotic idea that she and I belonged together. I told her that if she continued to behave like a silly child it would ruin what had been a good friendship between us, and she calmed down eventually. I stayed for a cup of coffee, and then I left.'

'But you didn't get home until very late.'

'I needed time to think, so I drove around for a while.' His sensuous mouth twisted in a somewhat savage smile. 'I was also furious with you, if you remember, because of that remark you made about being discreet about my affair with Delphine, and I decided to make you suffer a little.'

Understanding was beginning to filter through her confusion, but she was still plagued with uncertainty. 'I suppose you really were going to work late this evening, and that you had no intention of spending it with Delphine.'

His dark brows drew together in a frown as he stared at her taut, slender body with the green and gold curtains behind her. 'What the devil are you talking about?'

'Delphine telephoned about half an hour after you'd let me know you'd be working late, and she said you'd lied,' she explained, prodding at a wound which had not yet healed. 'She said she was expecting you any minute, and that you were going to spend the evening together. She said if I didn't believe her I was welcome to come along to her flat, but that she didn't think I was the type of wife who would want to embarrass myself as well as you by walking in on you when you were with another woman. And she was right about that, at least.'

'My God, that girl's been doing nothing but try to cause trouble!' Rollo exploded convincingly. 'I admit that I used her a little to make you jealous, but she had no right to call you and tell you I was going to spend the evening with her, because there's absolutely no truth in it!'

'I know that now,' Sherry admitted, drawing a careful breath, 'but I believed it earlier this evening and, believing it as I did, I was so confused when you walked into the house that I couldn't even begin to think straight.'

'Come here, Sherry.' His face was grave as he patted the bed beside him, and Sherry obeyed him, seating herself close to him so that she faced him. 'I have a lot of explaining to do, and there's no better time than the present,' he said, taking her hand in his and pressing a thrilling little kiss into her palm. 'When I left for the Antarctic two years ago I knew I loved you, but I couldn't accept that something like that had happened to me. I'd never believed in love before, but it took me two months away from you to finally make me realise how much you actually meant to me, and I wrote to you immediately, telling you how I felt. I asked you to ignore what I'd said before, and to wait for me.'

Her pulses leapt wildly. Could she believe him, or was this merely a prelude to more agony?

'I never received that letter.'

'I know you didn't,' he confirmed grimly, staring down at her hand which had become lost in his. 'It was returned to me some weeks later marked "address unknown".'

'Oh, God!' she croaked. If only she had known! If only she had waited instead of leaving Cape Town in such a hurry!

'The only thing I could do after that was to sit out my time in the Antarctic,' he continued in that grim voice that matched his expression. 'When I returned to Cape Town I spent more than three agonising months searching for you, but you'd left no trace. Not even Brenda and Jonathan knew where I could get in touch with you.'

'Brenda knew,' she confessed with difficulty, 'but I'd made her promise not to tell you if you asked.'

'Why?' he demanded, the expression on his ruggedly handsome face darkening into something close to anger, and it made her bow her head with guilt and remorse.

'You'd given me no reason to believe that your interest in me was of a lasting nature, and I didn't want you to know that I'd had your child because I knew you would feel obliged to marry me,' she explained, and her mouth curved in a cynical smile. 'Which is exactly what you have done.'

'You don't really believe that, do you?' he demanded softly, his hands framing her face and forcing her to meet his probing blue gaze. 'Not after everything I've just told you?'

She looked into his eyes and saw things there which she was still too afraid to accept. She tried to smile, but her lips started to quiver, and hot tears filled her eyes. 'I don't know what to believe any more!'

'My God, don't cry!' he groaned, gathering her roughly into his arms and crushing her so fiercely against his wide chest that she could scarcely breathe.

'I'm sorry, I—I can't help it,' she sniffed in a muffled voice, then his mouth found hers and he kissed her with a gentle passion until the tears stopped flowing.

His eyes burned into hers in a way that held her motionless in his arms and mentally suspended over a chasm, and when he spoke his voice was harsh, and yet vibrant with emotions that were fathomless.

'Haven't you realised yet that I love you, that I'm crazy about you, and that when I saw you again at Jonathan's house that night I could think of nothing else but taking time off from the busy schedule I was involved in to see you again, to talk to you, to tell you how much I cared, and to beg you, if necessary, to give me the opportunity to make you love me again?'

Those long awaited words released a flood of happiness so immense that she trembled with the force of it, and she flung her arms about his strong neck to bury her damp face against his shoulder. 'Oh, Rollo . . . if only I hadn't run like a coward back to Kromrivier!'

'You'll never know how I felt when I arrived at the hotel and found you'd gone,' he groaned against her hair while his hands moved in a groping caress across her back. 'I was in a fury when I followed you to Kromrivier, but it was nothing compared to what I felt when I discovered that you'd had my child. I think I went a little crazy then. I decided I was going to make you pay for all the agony I'd suffered, and it was as if you'd put a weapon in my hands with which to hurt you when you dredged up that ridiculous story that I was in love with Delphine and had wanted to marry her.'

'It *did* hurt. It hurt more than you'll ever know.'

'I wonder why?' he demanded mockingly, and she pushed him a little away from her to look up into his face.

'Because I still love you,' she said crossly. 'And don't tell me you didn't know that!'

'I guessed, but I wasn't sure.' His eyes crinkled at the corners in a faintly mocking smile. 'You've become very good at hiding your feelings, my darling, and I don't mind admitting that you had me scared at times.'

'I love you, Rollo,' Sherry murmured huskily, stroking the nape of his neck tenderly and sliding her hands across his wide shoulders. 'I love you very much,' she added, her grey eyes smoky with the extent of her happiness.

'What about Gordon Shaw?' Rollo demanded jealously.

She shook her head. 'I could never have married him, I'd never stopped loving you . . . not once, and marrying someone else was simply out of the question.'

She leaned forward, letting her mouth and her tongue explore his warm throat, his shoulder, and his hair-roughened chest. She tasted the salt of his skin, loving it, and a new hunger erupted deep down inside her as she trailed her seeking mouth down to caress his male nipple with the tip of her tongue.

'My God, Sherry, where did you learn to do that?' he groaned thickly, his hands tightening on her shoulders.

'You know damn well you taught me everything I know,' she answered jerkily, undoing the belt of her robe and allowing his impatient hands to do the rest.

He pulled her down beside him, his mouth seeking hers with a hunger that matched her own. His thighs were hard against her own, and his hips moved against hers in an erotic arousal that inflamed her. She slid her hands down his back to his hips, delighting in the play of muscles beneath his smooth skin, and she felt him grow taut with a heated desire when she pressed closer to him with a primitive longing which she could not suppress.

'I love you, Sherry,' he groaned against her mouth while his fingers expertly stroked the hardened peaks until the pleasure of his touch was almost a pain. 'I've never wanted any woman as much as I want you, and I'm never going to let you go out of my life again.'

'I like the sound of that very much,' she murmured against his mouth, her voice slurred and husky with emotion. 'I've never wanted to share my life with anyone else but you.'

They made love with a consuming passion as if there were not enough hours left in the night to express their love in sufficient ways, and later, when she curled up contentedly against his hard, male body with her head on his shoulder, she felt a strange new tranquillity wash over her that soothed away the two years of anguish as if it had never been.

They were soulmates again. They had both recognised it from the start, and they would never forget it in the future. They were as one, in mind, soul and body . . . until death and beyond.

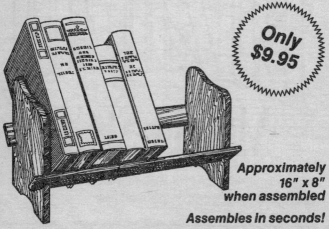

The passionate saga
that began with SARAH continues in the compelling,
unforgettable story of

Elizabeth

MAURA SEGER

In the aftermath of the Civil War, a divided nation—and two
tempestuous hearts—struggle to become one.

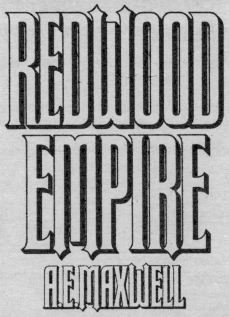

Harlequin Intrigue
Adopts a New Cover Story!

**We are proud to present to you
the new Harlequin Intrigue cover design.**

Look for two exciting new stories each month, which mix a contemporary, sophisticated romance with the surprising twists and turns of a puzzler . . . romance with "something more."

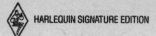

CAROLE MORTIMER

JUST ONE NIGHT

Hawk Sinclair—Texas millionaire and owner of the exclusive
Sinclair hotels, determined to protect his son's inheritance.
Leonie Spencer—desperate to protect her sister's happiness.

They were together for just one night.
The night their daughter was conceived.

Blackmail, kidnapping and attempted murder add suspense
to passion in this exciting bestseller.

The success story of Carole Mortimer continues with *Just
One Night*, a captivating romance from the author of the
bestselling novels, *Gypsy* and *Merlyn's Magic*.

**Available in March
wherever paperbacks are sold.**

WTCH-1